QUICK & EASY

The Quick Billionaires, Book 2

Whitley Cox

WHITLEY COX

DON'T FORGET

<u>Don't Forget</u>

Be sure to sign up for my newsletter to stay up to date on new releases, deals and more.
Sign up here —>https://whitleycox.myflodesk.com/newsletter
Become a Patreon Patron to get short stories, secondary character stories, favorite character update stories, exclusive cover reveals, exclusive excerpts from WIPs and more!
Support here —> https://patreon.com/authorwhitleycox

<u>A few other books by Whitley Cox</u>
The
Single Dads of Seattle
Grab book 1 here
https://books2read.com/HBTSD-SDS
*

The Quick Billionaires
Grab book 1 here
Quick & Dirty
https://books2read.com/QDirty-QBS
*

The Harty Boys

Grab book 1 here
Hard Hart
https://books2read.com/HH-HB
*

The Young Sisters
Grab book 1 here
Not Over You
https://books2read.com/not-over-you
*

Love to Hate You
https://books2read.com/Love2HateYou

For Authors Jeanne St. James and Erica Lynn.
My sisters from other misters, my people, my bitches.
This one is for you.
And also, in your faces, because I can so write a novella.
Not all my books wind up being 100,000 words.
Xoxo
Love you, Ladies.

CONTENTS

CHAPTER I

Heather

Wasn't it supposed to rain at a funeral?

It seemed every movie that had a funeral scene took place in the rain. All the guests wore black and clutched big black umbrellas while the rain masked the tears that slipped endlessly down their cheeks; the gray clouds in the sky mimicked the dark mood in everyone's hearts.

But it wasn't raining today. Not even a cloud in the damn sky. What the hell?

Heather Alvarez smoothed down the skirt of her charcoal gray lace dress (she just couldn't do black, even today) and stepped out of her Volkswagen Jetta. The warm April sun hit her cheeks at the same time a gust of wind ruffled the hair on the back of her neck.

She loved spring.

Her dad had loved spring, too.

"There you are," said her mother, Rosemary, coming out of their family's Puerto Rican restaurant, Hola, Amigos. "I was beginning to worry."

Heather offered her mother a small smile as she swung her purse over her shoulder. "Sorry, Mama. There was an emergency at work. You know how busy tax season can get." Heather bent down and planted a kiss on her mother's cheek before following her through the full parking lot to the front doors. "Have you needed my help? Or did Lena and Aunt Florence show up?"

Rosemary's hand fell to her daughter's back, bringing the scent of cumin and garlic and very subtle lavender. Her mother always smelled like cumin and garlic from the restaurant and lavender from her favorite shampoo.

She rubbed Heather's back affectionately, maternally. "We've had loads of help. Don't worry, sweetheart. Besides, you were here setting up all last night. What time did you finally get to bed?"

Heather dismissed the question with a shrug.

Rosemary let out a rattled sigh and glanced up at her daughter. Her pale blue eyes were glassy and her strong jaw tight. "This is what he wanted. He didn't want anybody crying over him. He wanted a party. So, we're going to give him a party."

Heather swallowed past the hard lump in her throat and looped her arm around her mother's slender shoulders, tugging her in tight. "I know, Mama. We're going to throw him the best celebration of life imaginable. Blow the roof off the place."

Rosemary chuckled and pulled open the door to the restaurant. Voices, loud and cheerful, greeted them. She met her daughter's eyes one more time before tossing on a giant smile. "Show time."

"Heather!" half a dozen or more people cheered as she stepped inside the bright and spacious restaurant. Tables had been pushed to the side and chairs lined up in rows. A podium stood front and center below the sign for half-price daiquiris on Mondays, and a small table with the picture of Eduardo Luis Gomez Alvarez sat next to it. Food, piled high, dressed the tables, while beer, local and imported, nestled tightly into ice buckets. Yes, her dad certainly knew how to throw a party, even in the afterlife.

Just like her mother was, Heather slowly made the rounds of all the guests, accepting condolences and sympathy, hugs and hand pats. Everyone had a story to tell about her father, all good, most funny. And Heather listened. She nodded. She cried. She laughed. By the time the minister announced the start of the sermon, Heather was exhausted, all cried out and ready to go home.

But she couldn't.

Her mother needed her. It was just the two of them now, and she needed to take care of her mom, be there for her. Hold her.

She took her seat in the front row, her mother on her left, her mother's best friend, Lena, on her right. Her mother's sister, Heather's Aunt Florence, sat on the other side of Rosemary, their hands clasped tight. Slowly, the noise in the restaurant subsided as people took their seats, the din of conversation and the scraping of chair legs on tile receding with the clearing of the minister's throat.

Heather spun around to take in all the people who had come to say "goodbye" to her father, to celebrate him and what he meant to the community. She absorbed their love, allowed it to bolster her own. Her father had meant everything to her, and in the blink of an eye—a heart attack at the dinner table when they were out for her birthday three weeks ago—he was gone.

It was a packed house. Standing room only and well over the legal limit of patrons for the restaurant. But they'd closed it for the day, put up signs and purchased special permits. If Eduardo Alvarez did anything, he did it aboveboard and he did it right. She was just about to turn back to the front when a big body sneaking in at the back caught her eye. The entire atmosphere in the restaurant shifted, and oxygen left Heather's lungs as she watched him slowly edge his way behind people, sticking to the shadows and the back of the room. He was tall. Perhaps taller than she remembered and bigger, too. His shoulders and chest were broader, and the way his dress pants hugged his thighs told her he still liked to work out and probably ride his mountain bike.

All the moisture left her mouth as she continued to follow him with her eyes. His head was down, and when he accidentally bumped someone, he was quick to apologize and move on. Eventually, he found a safe space next to the bar, quietly ordered a drink, then stood back, leaning the wide expanse of his back against a wooden column. He tipped his drink up, revealing a very expensive-looking watch at his wrist. His suit was tailored to perfection and high quality, too. Heather didn't know much about fashion or designers, but she knew that thing wasn't from JCPenney. His impossibly deep blue eyes closed, and his throat undulated on a swallow as he brought the belly-warming amber liquid into his mouth.

Heather swallowed, too. Fuck, he was still as drop-dead gorgeous as she remembered, as she dreamed. He still hadn't noticed her, so she took an extra moment to check him out. His swath of dark hair was shorter now, tamer, though it still had that unruly wave to it at the front. He never had been able to control the curl. But she'd loved it. Loved twirling her fingers around and around the silky soft strands as he laid his head in her lap and they watched movies. His gaze shifted, and suddenly his eyes lasered in on her.

A gasp escaped her before she could stop it, and immediately Heather spun back around in her seat. Her mother squeezed her hand, then patted the top with her other hand. "You okay, sweetheart?"

Heather swallowed again. "Yeah, Mama. I'm fine." Even though she was anything but. The back of her neck prickled and heated from his stare. She knew he was staring. Just knew it. His gaze had always been fierce. Had always stripped her bare and made her submit to his will.

I can't turn around. Willpower, girlie, willpower. Ah, fuck it.

She craned her neck around to catch another glimpse, and sure enough, he was zeroed in on her like a dog with a bone. The corner of his sexy mouth crooked up into a sad half-smile. His head shifted in an almost indiscernible nod.

The minister cleared his throat again, forcing Heather to spin back around. Her chest tightened and her gut knotted. The minister opened up his book and began. But Heather didn't hear a damn word. She was too focused on the voices in her head, on the memories that involved the impeccably dressed man at the back of the room. Gavin McAllister, the love of her life, and the boy who broke her heart.

CHAPTER 2

Gavin

Jesus fuck, she looked better than ever. Sexy as hell with her new hairstyle. The sleek dark bob that shimmied around those slender shoulders and brushed the neck he loved to kiss. He'd always had a thing for her neck. Something about how long and soft it was. The way it smelled, tasted. The feel of her pulse beating against his lips, faster and faster as he brought her closer to climax. God, he never could get enough of feeling her pulse race as he made her come. Never. Those cries still haunted his dreams each and every night. He compared other women's cries of ecstasy to hers as he took them between the sheets, but they never held a candle to her.

Gavin hoped she wouldn't see him until after the service, during the "party" part of the celebration of life. But when he'd caught her watching him, a part of him had been happy to know she'd recognized him, that he hadn't changed so much she didn't even know who he was.

Because inside he'd changed a lot. Inside he was a completely different man than the boy she'd known ten years ago, the boy who had pursued her until she'd relented, popped her cherry and stolen her heart. The boy who had promised that they'd be together forever and their long-distance relationship would work. The boy who had broken her heart over the phone, the coward who had heard her wracking sobs even in his dreams weeks later, but never called to check on her. Not once.

He wasn't that boy anymore. He wasn't that coward. He wasn't that asshole who wanted the freedom to party and sleep with whatever woman he wanted while away at college, rather than stick out the long-distance relationship with a great girl back home. No. He'd grown the fuck up. He'd grown the fuck up a while ago, but only now did he finally believe he might be worthy again of her love.

The sermon was nice. People near and dear to Eddie got up and spoke about him. Spoke about the kind man Gavin remembered fondly. He was a man who would give you the shirt off his back if you needed it, a man who helped his employees move, lifting the boxes himself, a man who gave all the leftovers from the kitchen each day to the homeless. This was the man they were mourning. A friend to all. A hero, and a man Gavin had considered a father.

Gavin's dad had skipped town when Gavin was two, going out for diapers and never coming back. His mother had tried her hardest to be both mom and dad, doing the best she could. But it was tough. She was a pediatric nurse and worked long hours, often through the night, which left ample time for Gavin to fall in with the wrong crowd and get up to no good. Never caught, but often close, he'd started doing some petty theft. Candy bars and gum, movies and DVDs. He'd gotten good at it, too. It wasn't until he decided to sneak into the back of a restaurant to try to steal a case of Corona beer that he was caught.

"I wouldn't do that if I were you," the deep voice with just a hint of a Spanish accent said in warning. "Not without a bag of limes, anyway. You can't drink Corona without a lime."

Gavin spun around. He'd almost made it out the back door scot-free. He froze. The man was huge. At least six foot one with dark hair, dark eyes, tanned skin. He had a big bushy mustache and a faint pink scar through his left eyebrow.

He's going to kill me.

The man took a few steps forward. "How old are you, son?"

Gavin swallowed. "S-sixteen."

The man nodded. "What's your name?"

"Gavin."

He took a few more steps, then held out his hand. "I'm Eddie and this here is my restaurant. Can I ask why you're stealing from me?"

Gavin didn't have an answer. And he didn't think "because stealing is fun" was one Eddie would accept. So instead, he simply stood there like moron.

Eddie took one more step forward, his hand still outstretched. He nodded at his hand and finally Gavin was forced to put the case of beer down and shake the man's hand.

"Now," Eddie started, "seems to me a boy has too much time on his hands if he's slipping into the back of restaurants stealing shit. Do you have a job?"

Gavin shook his head.

Eddie pulled his hand away and slapped Gavin on the back, guiding him deeper into the kitchen. "You do now. We need a busboy. You know how to clear a table and wipe it clean?"

Gavin nodded.

"Good." Eddie grabbed a white apron off a hook and shoved it into Gavin's hands. "Put that on and head out front. There are three tables that need clearing. You have any questions, you ask me or Hettie, got it?"

Before Gavin had a chance to answer, he was pushed through turquoise saloon doors and out into a Puerto Rican restaurant, salsa music playing while the mouth-watering smell of cumin and cayenne filled his senses.

Those same familiar smells hit him again just now as he rejoined the present. Soft Latin music played in the background, and the decadent aroma of cumin and cayenne, chili and garlic, cilantro and lime made his entire mouth fill with water and his stomach grumble. He hadn't eaten since breakfast, and that had consisted of a protein shake in the car on the way to the airport. He was famished.

Making his way over to the buffet table, he began to build a plate. God, he loved the food here. No matter where he went in New York, he couldn't find anybody that made an empanada like Eddie did. He piled three onto his plate, along with refried beans, guacamole, chips, salsa, and a heaping spoonful of arroz con gandules y lechón. Fuck, it'd been ages since he'd had Eddie's arroz con gandules y lechón. He added one more scoop for good measure.

He tucked a beer from the ice bucket under his arm, grabbed a napkin and fork, then headed off to find an empty seat. If he was going to win back the girl of his dreams, it was best done on a full stomach, and Eddie's beef turnovers and yellow rice and pigeon peas with roasted pork was a great way to start.

CHAPTER 3

What the fuck was he still doing here? She thought for sure Gavin would stay for the minister's sermon, and the stories, but she didn't expect him to stick around and eat. And holy fuck, was he eating. She was busy chatting with her friend Amber from the gym, but from where she sat, she had a perfect view of Gavin. Alone, at a table built for six, he inhaled his food as if he hadn't eaten in days, if not weeks. A small smile tickled her lips. He hadn't changed. He'd always been a big eater. The first time her parents invited him over for dinner, he'd surprised the hell out of them as he put away three burgers in one sitting, then had room for watermelon and a piece of Key lime pie. Her dad used to say Gavin had a hollow leg.

Maybe he was just happy to finally be eating her father's food again. He'd always loved the empanadas. They were her favorite, too.

Maybe you should have come back for a visit, you fucker. Wouldn't have had to wait ten years to taste one again.

Resentment and anger percolated in her veins while she spoke with Amber. Amber and her partner, Will, had been out for dinner with Heather and her family and friends the night her dad had a heart attack. Even Will, an ER doctor, couldn't save him in time. It meant a lot to Heather that they'd come to the service to support her. Amber was saying something about their kickboxing instructor, but Heather wasn't listening. Her eyes were focused on the man swigging his beer across the room instead. His big hand wrapped tightly around the neck of the bottle as he tipped it up.

She said her goodbyes to Amber and Will before making her way over to the buffet table. She eyed the food, but as delicious as she knew it to be, she wasn't hungry. Instead, she took a sip of her piña colada and hummed at the sweet, coconutty flavor with just the perfect splash of rum. Mike behind the bar knew how to mix them up right. But of course he did; Heather had taught him how.

She licked her lips and closed her eyes. How much longer did she have to stay? How much longer was *he* going to stay?

When she opened her eyes, her heart stopped. There he was, standing in front of her. All six foot two of him. A dark, neatly trimmed scruff hugged his chiseled cheeks, only adding to his ruggedness, while his blue eyes twinkled, fathomless and dark. There was an energy between them, a low hum beneath her skin, that had always been there. From day one, he'd made her body quiver, and with his body this close to hers, once again it was back. Like a subtle charge of electricity, it prickled and sizzled, making the hair on her arms stand up straight.

"Hettie."

Her whole body stiffened from the use of her nickname. Nobody called her that anymore. She was Heather Alvarez. Well, actually, Heather Luisa Maria Caterina Alvarez. Her father had wanted Louisa Maria and her mother had wanted Heather, so they compromised and then tacked on one more name for good measure. But "Hettie" had been her nickname growing up. He'd called her that as soon as they started dating. She'd loved her nickname since it was a family one. But when she no longer heard it from him, no longer heard his voice, dark, deep and demanding, saying her name as if it were a magic spell, her heart had shattered.

"Hettie." He said it again.

She'd wondered if he was going to show his face. A part of her had expected it. Hell, a part of her had hoped he would. She'd been curious. Though that's not to say she didn't check him out on social media from time to time. But he kept a low profile, so she didn't know much. He had a sexy, expensive-looking motorcycle and what looked to be a Ferrari, but then those could have belonged to a friend, too. Didn't mean he didn't look sexy as hell straddling the bike or sitting behind the wheel of the candy-apple-red 458 Spider. But as far as she knew, he hadn't been back to Seattle in ten years. Not once. And now, on the day of her father's celebration of life, he had the balls to walk into the restaurant and use her nickname.

She was determined not to let him see the hurt. He only deserved anger. Even though the anger had long dissolved, leaving nothing more than a hollow ache where her heart had once been.

"It's Heather," she said dryly.

His lips, those plump, soft, sensuous lips that she still had fleeting dreams about, curled up on one side into a lazy half-smile. "You'll always be Hettie to me."

Swallowing, she narrowed her eyes. "Only *he* is allowed to call me Hettie."

Like an idiot he spun around and looked behind him. "Who?"

Fixing him with her best you're-dead-to-me-stare, she replied, "The old Gavin."

And with that, she showed him her back and headed off to go speak with somebody, anybody, as long as it wasn't Gavin McAllister.

She hadn't made it very far before a warm hand and long fingers curled around her bicep, bringing her to a stop. Betraying her brain, her body sang in the heat of his palm. Once again she was back where she thought she'd be forever, in his arms. *Ha.* Oh, how wrong and naïve she'd been.

"Hettie," he said again, spinning her around to face him. "I want to talk."

"It's Heather," she gritted.

Disappointment clouded his face. "*Heather.* Can we talk … *please?*"

She shook her head and made to jerk out of his grasp. "I don't see what there is to talk about. It's been ten years, Gavin. I've moved on. So should you."

He reared back as if he'd been smacked, and hurt colored his eyes. "Y-you're seeing someone?"

Why was that such a big deal or surprise? She wasn't seeing anybody; she was single, but he didn't need to know that. What, did he think she'd wait around ten years, celibate and holed up in her apartment with twelve cats, waiting for him to one day come knock on her door and ask for forgiveness? Fuck him. She'd dated plenty over the last ten years. Even had a few boyfriends. The last one, Aaron Steele, had lasted nearly two years. But he was a Navy SEAL and always off on a mission, so in the end they'd called it quits. She couldn't do long distance, not again.

Heather lifted one shoulder. "So what if I am? It's none of your business who I see or what I do."

With his free hand he reached up and scratched the back of his neck. He always did that when he was nervous or unsure of what to say next. But the fingers of his other hand remained tight around her bicep.

"Where is he, then?" he finally asked, newfound confidence flashing in his eyes.

She let out a weighted sigh. "What do you want from me, Gavin?"

"I want to talk. Please? Give me five minutes of your time. Then you can tell me to fuck off."

Saved by the music. Over in the corner, Aunt Florence was busy fiddling with the stereo while Heather's mother wandered into the middle of the room. The music jerked and glitched, but then finally Florence figured it out, and a new tune, a sexy, sultry tune, burst loudly from the speakers.

"It was Eddie's request," Heather's mother started, "that his life be celebrated and not mourned. That we dance and party, we drink and be merry, rather than cry and wallow. He wanted dancing, lots and lots of dancing. And he was specific enough to say he wanted Hettie to dance."

All eyes zoomed to Heather standing in the corner next to Gavin, his fingers still wrapped tightly around her arm. Heat flooded her chest and crept up her neck into her cheeks.

"Remember how you and Gavin used to dance on Saturday nights here?" Rosemary asked, loud enough for everyone to hear.

How could Heather forget? It'd been one of the most incredible moments of her life. Her father's family had moved from Puerto Rico to Seattle when her dad was twelve. They'd started out in California but eventually settled in Seattle. After a stint in the police force, but forced into early retirement after a gunshot to the hip, her dad had opened up the restaurant when Heather was eight. He'd embraced all things Puerto Rican, pulling from his family's recipes, having decorations and paraphernalia sent up from his hometown. He wanted Hola, Amigos to be as truly Puerto Rican as he could make it. And that passion had carried over into Heather's house growing up as well. He spoke Spanish with her when he could, taught her to read it and write it, and eventually, when the dance bug bit her after a family vacation back to Puerto Rico when she was thirteen, she enrolled in salsa lessons. Through the years, she'd gotten quite good, won a few competitions, danced in the odd show, but she'd never found a partner who challenged her. Who made her better. She was always being given new partners and forced to train them because she was that good. But that wasn't what she wanted, what she needed.

Until Gavin, that is. From the moment he'd walked through those saloon doors, he'd been after her. But she'd resisted. She'd liked him all right. Knew him from school, knew him as a bad boy, one who skipped classes and smoked cigarettes behind the library. And she'd had a crush on him since the day he'd bumped into her in the hallway and mumbled a half-assed "sorry," but she couldn't let him know that. He was a bad boy, and as much as she wanted him, she knew he wasn't right for her. So, she turned down his advances for weeks, months, until that one fateful night when he must have heard her whining to her mother about losing another dance partner. He'd stepped up, offering to dance with her. She'd laughed at him, laughed in his face. But he'd been dead serious.

"I'm a fast learner," he said, mopping up a root beer spill on an empty table. "When's your competition?"

"A month," she said snidely.

"I can do it. We can do it. We'll train every day. I'll practice at home."

She gave him a curious look. "Why?"

"Because I like you. Your dad gave me a chance and helped turn my life around. I'm doing well in school, not skipping class or smoking anymore. I owe him. And if owing him means helping you, I'll do it." A wry smile tugged on his plump lips. "Plus, it's an excuse to touch you and hold you. And isn't salsa like a super sexy dance?"

She'd rolled her eyes and plopped a tray full of dirty dishes on the table he was wiping. "Twelve-fifty-six, Tremway Avenue, 4:15 tomorrow. If you're late, you're out." Then she walked away, smiling ear-to-ear as soon as she was through the saloon doors and knew he couldn't see her.

He'd been right. He was a fast learner. An incredibly fast learner. In less than three weeks he knew all the moves and was even helping her with her form. They'd practiced every day, watched videos and went to watch the experts at a salsa club downtown. On weekends they practiced twice a day, before work and after, until the day of the competition came around and they'd wowed the crowd and taken home third place. It was then, after all that hard work and training, time spent together swaying and gyrating, shifting and twirling that she finally saw the real Gavin.

Heather's mother's voice snapped her back to the present. Everyone in the restaurant was staring at Heather and Gavin off in the corner, her arm in his hand, their faces flushed. "Hmm, sweetheart?" Rosemary prodded. "Remember how good you two were together?"

Not subtle at all there, Mom.

Heather snorted.

"Your father asked that if Gavin were present that the two of you dance."

He did fucking not.

Claps whirled and built around the room and the music volume increased, until before Heather knew it, Gavin was removing his suit jacket, tossing it onto a nearby chair, and pulling her out to the makeshift dance floor, his hands in hers, strong, powerful and demanding.

"You don't have to do this if you don't want to," he said as his arm wrapped around her waist and he tugged her close. They were groin to groin, and the dash of a smile across his outrageously handsome face said he was well aware of it, too.

"You know as well as I do I don't have a fucking choice," she said through clenched teeth.

The music stopped and restarted. He raised her hand in the air with his, and his other hand at her back held her firmly against him. "You always have a choice, Hettie. I just hope after this you'll *choose* to talk to me."

"I have nothing to say to you, Gavin."

As the music picked up, he assumed his role in the dance and slowly, sensuously trailed his fingers down her arm. Plinks and plucks of the guitar, followed by a heavy hand on the bongos, stirred memories in Heather she had pushed down deep in an attempt to forget. And when the beat picked up and Gavin spun her out, only to pull her back into his chest, it all came flooding back. The feeling of being in his arms, dancing with him, kissing him, making love to him, it hit her like a dam breaking, and it was all she could do not to crumble to the ground in a heap of tears.

He must have noticed the look of terror on her face; dipping his mouth next to her ear, he murmured, "Forget you hate me just for now and finish the dance for your mother. Then we'll talk and you can release the venom."

Fury quickly replaced the pain in her heart, and she shot him a look that she hoped might just pop his head off. "I've already forgotten who I'm dancing with. I don't even know who he is."

CHAPTER 4

Gavin

Ouch! He'd deserved that.

Man, his Hettie could pack a wallop of a punch, even with her words. Always could.

But as he spun her around and around on the floor, ground his pelvis against hers, made her ride his leg, he couldn't deny their chemistry. They'd always had it. Since the moment she'd rolled her eyes at him when he asked her whether staff had to pay for fountain soda or if it was free, he'd been smitten. And from there it only got better. Their banter and conversations were what made him get up every morning excited to go to work after school. Seeing Hettie, talking with Hettie, impressing Hettie consumed his every waking thought.

And yet he'd still ended up breaking her heart.

He pulled her into him again against his knee. The skirt of her dress rose up, and he could feel the heat of her against his leg. His cock jerked inside his pants, and just to show her what she did to him, he pulled her tight against him.

Her eyes went wide, those big, beautiful, brown doll eyes he loved. He especially loved it when she was on her knees in front of him, his cock in her mouth, his hands in her hair as she took him to the back of her throat, watching him all doe-eyed and innocent, even though she was anything but. No, he'd taken her innocence, or rather she'd given it to him willingly one cold night in January after they'd gone out to a movie and then back to his place. His mother had been at work on a night shift, and they had the house to themselves. It'd hurt her, she hadn't gotten off, and she'd cried a bit from the pain, but then he'd ducked his head between her legs and made her forget all about the discomfort. They'd tried again the next day, and things had been better. By Valentine's Day, she was an orgasming machine, and he liked to consider himself a savant in the ways of female pleasure.

He snorted at the memory of his cocky teenage bravado. Thank God Heather had thought he was a beast in the sack, because as it turned out, he'd still had a lot to learn.

"What the fuck was that for?" she asked him, twirling out again.

"What?"

"The snort. You think this is funny? Getting shanghaied into dancing together in front of my friends and family, all to appease my dead father?"

His face sobered. "No. Well ... maybe a little." But he didn't miss the rosy glow to her cheeks or the smile on her face as he spun her out. She dropped the smile when forced to face him again. But deny it all she wanted, she'd missed this. He'd missed this. "It's more of a turn-on than anything, don't you think? Stirring up memories. Your body, in that dress, those curves, that hair flipping around. Your cheeks are pink, your eyes are bright, you look just like you used to after we'd—"

"Don't!" she snapped. "Don't you fucking dare."

A big grin stretched across his face. "I'm just saying..."

"You're just saying nothing." Her breathing was labored. She definitely sounded like she was having sex now. Gavin's cock surged to life in his pants.

The song was coming to an end, and Gavin's heart rate picked up. He needed to get her alone, needed to talk to her, needed to apologize the way he should have years ago. Spinning her into his chest one more time, he looped his arm around her back and dipped her low. Like a pro, she arched deep over his arm, letting her head fall back, exposing that sexy-as-fuck neck. Ten years ago, he wouldn't have thought twice about kissing it. Hell, he'd have probably licked and nipped it too, crowd be damned. But instead all he could do was stare. Watch as it bobbed with her swallow and the vein along the side beat in time to his own heart.

Once again, clapping filled the restaurant when the song finally ended. Followed by hoots and hollers, whoops and catcalls. Even a few whistles.

Rosemary rushed forward and hugged them both, tears in her eyes and slipping down her cheeks. "Thank you, both. That was beautiful. Your father would be so proud." She glanced up at the ceiling, then quickly crossed herself. "He *is* so proud." She hiccupped, and fresh tears sprung from her eyes. Heather lunged forward to envelop her mother in another hug. Soon the music picked up again, and the dance floor filled with people. Heather and Rosemary moved over to the side of the room, still hugging, their bodies trembling as they both silently cried over the incredible man they'd lost.

Gavin knew he needed to give Hettie time. Time to celebrate her father properly, grieve with her mother. Then they'd talk. They *needed* to talk.

Always keeping her in sight, he wandered back over to the buffet table. There was one lonely beef empanada left on the plate and he swooped in, devouring it in four bites, groaning as he chewed.

"You always did love his empanadas," came a familiar female voice.

Gavin spun around, wiping his mouth with a napkin. "I haven't been able to find anyone who does them better, let alone come close."

Rosemary smiled, her eyes red and puffy from crying. "I know why you're here."

Gavin's eyes went wide. "Why am I here?"

She gave him a smug but sad smile. "I'm grieving, not stupid. Just know, if you break her heart again, I'll come after you and kill you myself, that is if Eddie's ghost doesn't get to you first."

Gavin wanted to throw his head back and laugh, but he knew better. Rosemary had always been feisty. That's where Hettie got her spunk. Not afraid to call a spade a spade or simply pick up a spade to bonk you over the head if needed.

Instead, he simply nodded. "I know. And I promise, I won't this time. If any hearts are going to be broken, it'll be mine."

That answer seemed to satisfy her, and she wiped beneath her eyes with a crumpled tissue from her pocket. "Good." She reached up, and he bent down for a hug. She was fragile and tiny in his arms, but she smelled like the home he remembered, even if it'd only been his home for a short time. Cumin and garlic with just the faintest hint of Rosemary's favorite lavender shampoo. He'd only lived with the Alvarezes for a few months, after his mother had died in a car accident shortly after Christmas before he graduated high school. Hettie's family had taken him in when he had nowhere to go. But they'd quickly become *his* family. Eddie had been like a father to him pretty much from day one, giving him a job and a chance to be a better person, while Rosemary clucked around him like a mother hen the moment he mentioned his mother worked nights. He'd never eaten dinner alone again. Thank God, Hettie had never been like a sister, though.

"I've missed you," Rosemary said into his shoulder.

Well if that didn't hit him in the solar plexus. Yeah, he'd missed them all, too. He'd been an asshole not coming back for all these years. And he hated himself that it took him ten years and the funeral of a man who'd been like a father to him to get his ass back.

But now that he was back, he was going to make the most of it. He was going to make things right.

Rosemary dried her eyes again when they separated, then with a final squeeze to his arm, she wandered off to go and speak with some of the staff.

As bopping as the dance floor was, with bodies swinging and twirling, spinning and dipping, the restaurant was also clearing out. What had been over one hundred people during the minister's sermon was now roughly a third of that. Only the diehard partiers and close friends of Eddie remained. Some of them Gavin recognized, regulars who had been coming in to the restaurant since he bused tables, while other faces were new. He scanned the crowd, looking for the only face that mattered.

He spotted Hettie over by the door, where she was getting her coat. *Shit!*

Snatching his jacket off the chair, he set off into a steady lope toward the door, determined not to let her leave without hearing him out. Her hand was on the door handle by the time he got to her.

"You're not leaving, are you?" Fear gripped him, and his pulse thudded in his ears.

She rolled her eyes. "I'm tired, Gavin. I was up all night setting this place up, then I had to work this afternoon. Tax season doesn't stop for bereavement. My mother said I could leave. I offered to stay; she shooed me away. I'm going home to bed."

That last word made his eyelids drop to half-mast and his cock spring up to a half-chub.

His hands enclosed around her fingers on the door handle. "We need to talk first. Please? I'm staying at the Windward Pacific Hotel. You can come there if you'd like."

Her eyes flared for a moment in surprise. Yes, he knew it was the most expensive hotel in the city, but after what he had to tell her, she'd understand why he was now in a position to stay at such a place.

"I'll go anywhere you say, Hettie."

As long as it's not to hell.

"I just really want, no, *need* to talk to you."

Exhaustion escaped her on a long, loud sigh. "Follow me home. We can talk there. I need to get out of this dress and these shoes."

She didn't wait for his answer, didn't even wait for a nod. Weary-eyed, with slumped shoulders, she pushed past him and opened the door. The sun was setting, and the way its rays caught the red highlights in her dark hair made his balls tighten. She was beautiful. A Latina angel in the heart of Seattle. The sway of her hips and the long lines of her legs as she headed to her car hypnotized him, and before he knew it, he was slipping the key of his rental into the ignition and following the love of his life back to her home, where she was going to either give him a second chance or stomp all over his heart. He hoped for the former but deserved the latter.

CHAPTER 5

What had she been thinking, inviting Gavin back to her place? That's right, she hadn't been thinking, or at least her brain hadn't been. Fuck, the way he'd spun her around on that dance floor, the sway of his hips, the thrust of his pelvis, the naughty glint in those sexy dark blue eyes. It was freaking foreplay, and he knew it. She'd been out of breath and wet by the time the song had ended, her breasts straining against the tight dress, desperate to be free. So that's why she'd invited him home. Not one brain cell had taken part in that decision; it'd been all libido.

As soon as the song ended and her mother gave her her blessing to flee, she'd been out the door, only he'd caught her. He always caught her. Heather figured if she made it out of the restaurant without Gavin noticing her, he wouldn't be able to find her and she could go home to take care of the hollow ache between her legs with her favorite vibrator. But nooooo, his ninja skills seemed to have been honed over the years, and he was on her like a dirty shirt, begging her to sit and listen to whatever spiel he figured would make her forgive him. Well, she would tell him and anyone else who would listen right now, nothing he could say would make her ever take him back, ever forgive him for breaking her heart and ending things the way he did, nothing.

But despite her conviction to never forgive Gavin McAllister, the low-down, selfish bastard, their dancing had turned her on something fierce. And as luck, or lack thereof, would have it, she was also single and hadn't been with a man in ages.

Fuck, was it coming up on a year? Yeah, must be.

So as she drove home, glancing far too much in the rearview mirror at him following behind her, she decided she was going to get the closure he never gave her. Get the breakup sex he owed her. Get her rocks off, have some orgasms and then kick his ass to the curb and never look back.

She hit the button for the door to her parking garage, and slowly it lifted. There were a few visitor spots, so Gavin grabbed one. She was out of her car first, walking around the back and admiring the sleek lines of his Audi RS7. Quite the rental. Last time she'd traveled anywhere, she'd been happy with the Ford Focus the rental company gave her. She didn't want to even think about how much that Audi was costing him per day. More than her mortgage probably.

"Nice car," she said smoothly, the click of her heels on the pavement drowning out the thud of her pulse in her ears.

He followed her to the elevator. "Thanks. It's a rental. But I have the same year and model back home, so it's a familiar drive."

Holy shit! What the hell did Gavin McAllister do for a living to be able to afford an Audi RS7, Ferrari and sexy motorcycle?

He ran a big hand through his thick, dark hair. Damn it, why did he have to go and be even sexier than she remembered? Why couldn't he have gained two hundred pounds, suffered from severe hair loss and adult cystic acne? That would have made things a lot easier. But no, he was handsomer than ever. Good thing he was still a crappy person on the inside. That would make tossing him out after sex a lot easier.

The elevator doors opened. They both stepped inside. Heather slid her key card into the slot, and the car began to rise.

"Nice. You in the penthouse or something?" he asked, rocking back on his heels and admiring the bright gold mirrored walls of the elevator car.

She shook her head. "No. Fifth floor of twelve. But the level of security in this place was appealing."

"Cool. Yeah, I have a key card to my place too."

She wanted to ask if he was in the penthouse of his condo, but she didn't want to give him the wrong idea that she was interested in him or his life. No. She wanted his body. She wanted his cock and perhaps his tongue and that was it. Once she got those things, had her merry way with them, he was going to be out the door. This needed to be quick, and this needed to be easy. There would be no pillow talk, no breakfast. Quick and easy breakup sex ten years later, that was all this was going to be.

So instead of asking the burning questions that seemed to be mounting rapidly in her brain, she put her head down and stared at her shoes.

The elevator dinged, and the door opened. She stepped out first and took a left.

"This is a nice building. Have you lived here long?"

Her pace was brisk. There was no time for chitchat. She needed him naked and gone before sunrise.

"A couple of years. It was a brand new building. I'm the first owner of my unit."

"Sweet. I can't wait to see it."

She slid the key into the lock and opened the door. Immediately she threw the overhead lights on in the kitchen, followed by one in the living room. Heather loved her condo. It was bright, east-facing, so it got lots of morning sun. Had a big balcony where she grew vegetables and flowers, two bedrooms, two bathrooms and a walk-in closet she could call a third bedroom and rent out if times ever got tough. She kept things minimal with very few knickknacks, and everything had a place and a purpose. She liked the clean look of white, so besides the odd pop of scarlet or dark gray, pretty much everything was white or another neutral shade.

"This is a really great place," Gavin said, toeing off his shoes and hanging up his coat near the door. He wandered into her living room and gazed out the big picture window that showcased the Space Needle all lit up. "Wow, quite the view."

She hung up her purse and coat. "I know. I love it. Though I haven't been up to the top of that thing in ages."

"Remember when we went up there for my birthday?"

Heather snorted and made her way into the kitchen. She opened up the cupboard with all the liquor and pulled out a bottle of scotch. "Hard to forget that cold January night. A lot happened."

He spun around with a big grin on his face, his saunter practiced and carefree as he approached her in the kitchen. "Yes, *a lot* did happen. A lot of wonderful things."

She poured them each two fingers of scotch, then slid one glass across the island to him. "Yes, well, as much fun as me getting my cherry popped in your twin bed on your birthday was, we're not sixteen anymore, and things have changed."

She tossed back the scotch like it was 7UP, then poured another two fingers.

"A lot has changed, you're right." He took a sip, eyeing her over the rim of his glass.

This time, Heather just took a sip. She rested the glass down on the island. "I'll be right back." Without even looking at him, she took off to the powder room just off the kitchen. A quick makeup check to ensure there were no raccoon eyes, followed by a wet wash cloth to her lady parts, and she was good to go. Steeling herself for a night of meaningless sex with her ex, she tossed back her shoulders and plastered on her best sexy smile before opening the door. "So, are we fucking or what? Because I need to get the hell out of this dress. It's way too tight after all those empanadas."

Gavin's chin nearly hit the floor. "I, uh ... that's not why I came over here, Hettie. I really do want to talk to you."

She rolled her eyes as she went on the hunt for the zipper of her dress. "I don't want to talk. I want to fuck. You owe me breakup sex. Hard to have it when you get dumped over the phone." She found the zipper on the side of her dress and began to pull it down. Before she knew what was happening, Gavin had raced over and his hand was on hers, halting her efforts to undress.

"If you take your dress off, I won't be able to concentrate on what I have to tell you. Please," he reached for her hand, "can we just go sit in the living room and talk?"

She shot him a look that said, "this better be good," before grabbing her scotch and letting him lead her around the island and into the living room. She took up residence on her cream-colored leather couch. The cashmere cushions behind her were silky soft, and she snuggled right in, curling her legs up under her.

Gavin sat beside her but gave them enough space that their legs weren't touching and his incredible manly scent wasn't driving her bonkers. The scotch was already working its magic into her limbs; a tingling warmth seeped out through her belly, warming her extremities and easing her overactive imagination. He took a sip of his drink before resting it on her zebrawood end table. He used a coaster, which surprised her—in a good way.

Taking a deep breath, he turned to face her. "I owe you more than an apology. I owe you an explanation. I owe you, well, fuck, I owe you my life. You, your parents, you all saved me. And I didn't go about showing my appreciation in the right way. I should never have ended things with you over the phone."

Her breath caught audibly, and his head shot up.

"Shit, sorry. I mean, I should never have ended things with you at all, but certainly not over the phone." Scrubbing a hand over his face, he closed his eyes for a moment.

His fingers made a raspy sound against his scruffy close-shaved beard, and all Heather could think about was about the sweet, sweet pain of whisker burn. On her lips, her cheeks, her neck, her nipples, her ...

Removing his hand, he opened his eyes. They were tired, but clear and bright with resolution. He continued on. "A lot happened that first year I moved to New York. A lot that I didn't tell anybody about. And when it all happened, I was really lost, and trying to manage a long-distance relationship just added to the mess of things. I didn't want to break up with you. But I was young and stupid, and I figured it would be easier ending it before I made a mistake, like got drunk one night and cheated on you."

"So you dumped me so you could go party and fuck without the guilt of a girlfriend back home?"

"Yes." Her eyes went wide. He shook his head emphatically. "Wait, no. But yes. All my friends were single, partying, hooking up. In some ways I felt like it was something you just needed to do, get out of your system before you have to grow up, get a job and settle down. So, yeah, to build on the horrible image you already have of me, that's part of the reason why I ended things."

Heather reached for her scotch and took a long, healthy sip. It went down smooth and easy. Her father always did know how to pick good scotch. She rolled the last sip around on her tongue for a few moments, considering Gavin's words.

They hurt.

They hurt a lot.

But there was some truth to them as well. She'd felt left out at college, too. While Gavin had gone off to Columbia on a full math scholarship, Heather had stuck around Washington state, attending the local college and getting a degree in accounting. She'd made friends quickly at school and went to parties most weekends, but despite how much she loved Gavin, she'd been envious of the girls dancing and making out, hooking up and dating. It seemed like a rite of passage. So she understood where Gavin was coming from, because after he'd dumped her and she allowed herself some time to grieve, she'd started dating and hooking up, partying and dancing. She experienced college to its fullest and had countless great memories to show for it.

Maybe they had been too young to be so committed. Maybe breaking up was the right thing?

"Shortly after Christmas that first year," Gavin continued, "I received a letter in the mail to tell me my father had died."

Heather nearly choked on the scotch. "Your dad? But I thought he ... "

Gavin nodded. "Nobody knew where he'd taken off to. Went out for diapers and never came back. That's the story my mom stuck to for years. But anyway, I received a letter saying that he died. I also received a check. Because turns out as terrible as he was at being a dad, he was just that apt at being a businessman. He'd accumulated over forty million dollars, and ten of those were on the check to me."

Now Heather's chin nearly dropped to her lap. "*Ten million dollars?*"

"Yeah. I also apparently have three half-siblings. Great business man, shitty dad, can't figure out a condom to save his life. That's Randall McAllister for you."

"Did he give them any money?"

"It was split four ways, so we each got ten mil."

"Have you met them?"

"I've met one," he said softly. "My older brother, Tate, lives in Tahiti. He owns a bunch of resorts there as well as holds shares in hotels around the world. He started bringing me in on the deals, too. We both own substantial shares in the Windward Pacific downtown. The guy's a billionaire. I have another brother who I've only spoken to on the phone or communicated with through emails. And we have a sister out there, too, but we haven't been able to track her down."

Holy shit. He hadn't told her any of this, none. Did her dad know? Her mother? Had they all been keeping Gavin's millionaire status a secret from her? Did he break up with her because he thought she was a gold digger and would spend all his money? The mere thought tasted acrid on her tongue. No, he knew her better than that, knew she didn't care about that kind of thing. She'd loved him when he was a poor orphan. She would have loved him as a millionaire too.

Heather was up and off the couch in a matter of seconds. She snatched the scotch bottle from the counter and brought it back over to the couch. After topping them both up, she sat back into the cushions. "Okay, so you're loaded now." She paused. "Wait, so the Harley Davidson and Ferrari are yours?"

He nodded. "Yeah." Now it was his turn to pause. A crooked grin caught on his lips. "How do *you* know I own a Harley and a Ferrari? Been snooping around on Google?"

Her face was hot. Shit! Stupid scotch causing her to not have an adequate working filter. How the hell was she going to get out of this one?

Rolling her eyes, she tipped back her glass and took a sip. "My mother may have shown me a photo or two of you in passing." She scoffed for good measure. "So, is that what you came here to tell me, that you're Richie Rich now?"

He took another sip before answering. "Not just that. I want you to know everything. The whole story. So, after I inherited the money from my dad, my life started spinning out of control. I suddenly could afford anything I wanted. I spent and spent and spent. Went on trips, rented a sweet apartment right across from Central Park. I lived the life of Riley for a good six months. Even though inside I was a mess. It wasn't until Tate got ahold of me about a year later—he flew to New York to meet up, and when he saw how I was living, he knocked some sense into me. He wasn't living in Tahiti at the time. He was living in South Korea running a hotel there. But he was saving his money, investing well. He had his eye on a rundown resort in Tahiti and was waiting for the price to drop just a little lower. When it did, he swooped in, bought it and turned it into one of the most luxurious resorts in the world."

Heather shook her head. Where the hell was Gavin going with this? Why was he blathering on about his billionaire big brother? Did Gavin live in Tahiti now, too? Was that going to be the big revelation?

"Okay ... " she said, not wanting the story to end, but more to just get to the point. She was still eager to get to that breakup sex, and the more scotch she pumped into her bloodstream, the more she wanted Gavin naked and inside her.

"Anyway, Tate didn't like the road I was on. Said I'd be broke in less than two years at the rate I was spending. So, he guided me with some investments. We bought up some real estate properties together, chose some good-looking stocks to put some coin into, then we sat back and watched my money grow. I gave up my apartment, moved back in with roommates, and I lived the life of a college student. I also found a passion. Playing the stock market became my new obsession. Watching the numbers spike and plummet became the best kind of high. I no longer cared about parties; I lived for the adrenaline rush of the New York Stock exchange every morning. It was better than coffee."

"That sounds like a horrible life," she said, with a head shake and sneer. "Money isn't everything."

A soft smile coasted across his face. "You're right, it's not. I flew to Tahiti a few months ago to see my brother. He's married and expecting a baby. He's a completely new man. Happier than I've ever seen him, at peace and in love."

"Good for him," she said quietly. "I'm glad he realized there is more to life than just money."

He nodded. "And he helped me realize it, too. He said I struggle to find a balance. He says Parker, his wife, is what balances him out. I was obsessed with spending and partying, then I became obsessed with *making* money and the stock market. Tate helped me see that I was wasting my life away obsessing over money and stocks. And truth was, I wasn't even happy in my job anymore. But I have an addictive personality, and like an alcoholic, I'd become dependent on it, and I saw no way out. I couldn't just get up one day and not check the Dow Jones. It'd become as a part of me as breathing."

She frowned. "That's really sad."

"Isn't it? But Tate helped me realize there is more to life than that. He sent me to a therapist while I was on the island, and she helped me realize that I've been so scared of turning into my dad and letting people down, I never let anyone get close enough to be able to let them down." His lips dipped into a frown. "Besides you, that is. I haven't let anyone else get close enough since you."

Affected by his words but not willing to let him see it, Heather hid her face with her glass and took a long drink. Jesus, this was information overload.

He must have taken her silence as an invitation to continue. "The therapist asked me what kinds of things make me happy, because we'd identified when I went to see her that I couldn't have been further from happy. She told me to close my eyes and think about the happiest moments in my life. Then she asked me who was there and what we were doing. All I saw when I closed my eyes was you. The two of us, dancing, laughing, kissing, making love. In every truly happy memory I have, you are front and center."

Heather sat there frozen.

Gavin pressed on. "I've quit my job. I actually quit it six months ago and have since been setting up a nonprofit organization that helps families without adequate funding or access to medical care get the help they need. It also helps people who can't afford expensive medications and prescriptions get what they need. I want to do something worthwhile with my money, with myself and my time. Tate figures by Christmas next year, if our real estate investments pay off the way he thinks they should, I'll be a billionaire or just shy of one."

Heather's mouth fell open and all the air left her lungs.

Billionaire?

CHAPTER 6

Gavin

Was she going to say anything? Was she having a stroke? He couldn't tell. The woman just sat there staring at him, wide-eyed, mouth open, speechless.

Well, what do you expect, numbnuts? You just dropped the B-word.

"Heather?" he prodded gently. "You okay?"

Finally, those big doe eyes of hers blinked a couple of times. "Y-yeah, I'm okay ... *billionaire?*"

He nodded. "Yeah. But maybe not. A billion is a lot of money, and our dollar ain't doing so hot at the moment. I could be a pauper by next Christmas instead of a billionaire. You never know."

Her snort made him smile. "Yeah, a *pauper*. I'm sure."

His smile grew wider. He loved how candid and blunt she was. Always had given him a run for his money, never took any of his shit or chiding. She'd made him work for her love and attention every step of the way. And then when he'd finally had her, he'd kicked her to the curb. God, he was such a dumb fuck back then.

But he was smarter now. Still not a genius, because it'd taken a therapist and his long-lost brother to knock some sense into him, but he was learning.

"So, I get to have breakup sex with a soon-to-be-billionaire then?" The last part came out as a giggle, and Gavin realized his sweet little Hettie was drunk. Had he ever witnessed her drunk before? She'd always been such a good girl, no drugs, no smoking, no drinking, good grades.

Her parents' angel.

His angel.

"Is that what you want from me?" he asked. He still had so much to say to her, so much to tell her, to ask her. But would it fall on deaf ears? Was she too drunk to understand that he was there to ask for another chance? To ask her to take him back and let him love her again?

She hiccupped and grinned. Her eyes held a glassy and glazed-over look, and her cheeks were a sexy rosy red. Fuck, she was stunning. He'd always loved her coloring. Dark hair, dark eyes, naturally tanned skin. She was a Latina goddess whom he'd never been able to get enough of. In all their years apart, he'd never met or been with a woman who tasted as sweet, or whose noises when she came made him come all the harder.

"You owe me that much, Gavin McAllister, billionaire extraordinaire," she said smoothly. Slowly, like a lithe feline temptress, she stood up. Her hand fell to her side, and her bottom lip snagged between her teeth. Without letting her gaze leave his eyes, she drew down the zipper of her dress; the sound of the metal teeth of the zipper was an erotic buzz in the pounding silence of the room. The fabric peeled away from her luscious skin, pooling at her feet in a heap of gray lace. She stood before him, a vision he'd dreamed about often. But she'd also changed in the last ten years. Her breasts had filled out and were perfect rounded handfuls, tucked up and pushed up in that sexy lace bra. Her hips were curvier and more feminine that he remembered, and her waist was a sensuous hourglass. Plenty to hold on to, if she gave him the chance.

Gavin swallowed hard and let his eyes rake the beauty before him. "God, Hettie, you're fucking perfect."

She stepped out of her dress and approached him. "If I was so perfect, why'd you break up with me?" Like the goddess that she was, full of grace, she stood over him. The black lace at the V of her thong tempted him. He ran his tongue between the seam of his lips. It was taking every ounce of his self-control not to jam his face between her legs and inhale her scent.

"Biggest fucking mistake of my life," he said through ragged breaths. He allowed his eyes to leave the apex of her thighs, and he found her staring down at him. Curiosity colored her face.

"Was it?"

How could she ask him that? Of course it had been. He'd been a wreck for months. The amount of times he'd called her, or almost called her, only to hang up before it started to ring ... But he just hadn't wanted to drag her into the mess of him figuring out the money, of his sudden wealth or what the hell to do with it. It's not that he figured she was a gold digger and after his cash, but money changed people, changed the way people treated you. So he'd figured the less people who knew about the money the better. Tate was a billionaire nobody knew about, and Gavin wanted to be the same. Keep his fortune a secret, maintain his anonymity and privacy.

Her head cocked to the side, and her eyes squinted at him, studying.

Pushing back into the couch, he ran his hand over his face again. "Fuck, Hettie. It was the hardest damn thing I ever had to do. I didn't *want* to do it. But I figured it was the best thing … for the both of us. I wasn't in a good state of mind to have a girlfriend. You were too innocent and sweet, and I knew I'd just fuck it all up at some point. I wanted to save you the heartache."

Her eyes burned into him. "My heart still ached, so you saved nothing."

Clenching his teeth until a dull pain thudded in his jaw, he looked up at her imploringly. "I know that now, and I'm sorry. I was young, stupid, selfish and fucked up. I'll never forgive myself for what I put you through."

She raked her teeth over her bottom lip, and the high cheekbones of her face sharpened. "Then apologize properly."

The temptation of her sweet skin, the urge to taste her was too much. Did she taste as good as he remembered? He reached out and grabbed her by the hips. Those sloe bedroom eyes of hers flashed wide in surprise as his fingers dug into the soft, plump skin of her ass and thighs. "Hettie," he started, "if I take you, I'm going to take you hard and all fucking night long. There won't be anything quick or easy about it. I've waited ten long years to be back inside you, to taste you, and now that I have you, I'm going to savor you."

Her throat bobbed on a heavy swallow, and those pouty lips of hers opened into a fuckable little *O*.

"Is this what you want?"

She nodded. "Yes."

"Am *I* what you want?"

Another nod.

Not wanting to waste another moment, and abandoning all resolve, he gripped the fabric of her thong and pulled, tearing it straight off. Her eyes widened at the snap against her skin. Tossing the ruined thong to the side, he brought his gaze back to her pussy. Fuck, suddenly he was starving. He wanted her in his mouth, wanted to hear her moans and feel her slickness coat his lips as she lost herself and deserted all composure.

To hell with gentle, he palmed her thighs and spread her legs wide before wrapping his hands around the firm cheeks of her ass and bringing her forward to thrust his tongue between her slick silky lips.

Heather gasped, but her shock was fleeting, and like a woman who knew what she wanted and wasn't afraid to take it, she let her hands weave their way into his hair and tugged. He groaned when she pulled on the ends. Yes, the pain. He loved the pain. He *deserved* the pain.

She was already getting wet for him and tasted even better than he remembered. Sweet like honey and so responsive. With each flick of his tongue over her clit, she gushed more sweetness out into his mouth, and he lapped it all up like a man who'd been wandering the desert, thirsty for days. Up through her creamy folds he swept his tongue, only to then draw her swelling clit between his lips, sucking until she trembled in his palms. He hadn't even pushed his fingers inside her, and already she was close.

Twiddling his tongue over her hood, he felt her body stiffen in his grasp. Her hands tightened in his hair, and she thrust her pelvis forward into his face as her climax claimed her. Beautiful moans and feminine gasps filled the room, but instead of easing off, he only attacked her cleft harder. More sucking, more licking, more flicking, until she shattered into a million beautiful little pieces against his lips when another orgasm took her by surprise.

Yes, Hettie. Yes, my angel. From here on out, all your orgasms will be mine.

More and more she bucked into his face, grinding her slit against his mouth and nose. His whiskers scraped her inner thighs and labia, but she either liked it or didn't seem to mind because she just kept pushing harder, taking what she wanted from him. Using his body as her plaything, for her pleasure. And he wanted her to. He wanted her to use him, to make herself feel good. He wanted Hettie, *his* Hettie to feel nothing but good when she was with him. Lord knows he'd made her feel fifty different kinds of shitty over the last ten years, and he had a lot to make up for.

When her second orgasm finally subsided, she went to pull away, but he held on tight and gave one long final sweep up between her soft, swollen folds. She shuddered beautifully in his arms. When he brought his head up, he smiled. Her eyes were closed, her cheeks a rosy red and her head lolled to one side. She was sated, fucked and ready for bed. Too bad she wasn't *thoroughly* fucked. No. That would take all night. He wanted to be inside her more than he wanted to breathe, and if she was willing, he'd take her any way, every way and as many times as humanly possible.

"Hettie?" Gavin said softly, quietly admiring the curves of her body while her eyes were still closed. When they'd been together, she hadn't waxed or shaved. Now, she was sporting a freshly manicured thin strip, and it called to him like a goddamn airport runway. He had to land his seven-inch 747, he just had to.

Slowly, languidly, sleepily, she lifted her eyelids, gazing down at him. A small, sexy smile crept to her lips. "Hi," she said softly.

A chuckle bubbled up in his throat. Fuck, she was just so sweet. "Hi."

"You're better at that than I remember."

"Yeah?"

Her grin grew wider, and she slowly dropped to her knees in front of him. She pushed his legs apart and positioned herself between his thighs. "I'm better at a few things too," she said huskily.

He swallowed. Fuck. Now was *not* a good time to be thinking about the love of his life and her lips wrapped around the shaft of someone else. He'd be a moron to assume she'd been celibate all these years. Hell, he knew for a fact she hadn't been. And lord knows he hadn't joined the priesthood. He'd gotten better at eating pussy since they were last together, because in the last ten years he'd eaten a lot of it. He'd been schooled and had perfected the craft. And now, after all those lessons and practice, it boiled down to tonight. He had to impress Hettie. Win her back. Apologize. Make her his again.

With slender fingers, she unzipped the zipper of his slacks. Fishing around in the hole, among the fabric of his boxers, she finally found what she'd been seeking. He'd grown hard as granite tasting her juices, and now seeing her there on her knees, he was about ready to explode in his pants. It was all too much.

A dewy bead of pre-cum glistened on the plum-hued crown of his cock, and he ached for her to lick it off as he dug his hands into the satiny tresses of her hair and reeled her in. Her cute little pink tongue darted out, and she did just that, laving at the crown, and swirling the pre-cum around the tip. He groaned, and his hips spasmed off the couch. God, she'd always sucked cock like a pro and swallowed every drop like it was a fine wine, but he had a feeling the vixen had perfected her skills over the years. He just needed to make sure he didn't blow his load too soon.

She took him into her mouth and immediately let him bottom out. Her throat contracted around the head, and his balls tightened in his slacks. Fuck. Shit. Damn. He was going to come.

Grabbing her by the shoulders, he pushed her off, his breathing ragged and his cock wet and shiny from her hot little mouth.

She looked up at him in confusion with those beautiful brown eyes, and his heart constricted in his chest.

"What's wrong?"

His head shook fast. "Nothing. I just ... I just don't want that right now. I want to please *you*. I want to worship *you*." He'd been a quick shot their first time together, too, lasted no more than two minutes, and although their sex life had improved over time, he didn't want their reunion sex to be quick, either. He wanted to savor Hettie, please Hettie until she was limp, boneless and begging for sleep.

She licked her lips. "But I want to." A sigh fled past her lips, and he was hit with the scent of liquor. She was still a little drunk.

Bringing her up to standing, he bent low and scooped her up into his arms. "I want to fuck you on your bed. Maybe later you can suck my cock, but I haven't had my fill of your sweet pussy." There were three closed doors before him as he crossed the living room. "Which one is the bedroom?"

Kicking her legs out with a girlish giggle, she looped her arms around his neck. "The one on the right." They were there in three long strides. He tossed her onto the bed hard enough to make her bounce. In no time at all, he was naked, hard as ever-loving fuck and desperate to be inside the love of his life. He had a strip of condoms in his pocket that he'd snatched from his car when he arrived at her house, and he had every intention of using the majority of them.

Standing at the foot of her bed, he gazed down at her, and holy shit! Gavin's jaw nearly hit the bed. She was propped up on the pillows near the headboard, naked from the waist down and watching him as two fingers flicked her clit and fucked her sweet little pussy. Her eyelids had drooped to half-mast, and she licked her lips again. Her gaze fell to the raging hard-on between his legs.

"You've been working out," she said lazily, her legs spread wide for him, showing off her slick, swollen lips.

His eyes raked her body. "So have you."

She lifted one shoulder cavalierly. "I still dance. I do spin and kickboxing. But you, how do you get abs like that?"

He ran his hand over his six-pack, one he'd worked hard to get. He'd hired a trainer and nutritionist, and they'd put him on the right path. He'd also taken up swimming and still enjoyed mountain biking when he had the chance. That first year in college, he'd gained fifteen pounds from all the drinking and shit food he'd been eating, so once Tate knocked some sense into him and told him to smarten the fuck up, he'd committed all the way.

Mimicking her shrug, he offered her a small smile. "Not sure. I woke up one day, and they were just there."

She rolled her eyes. All the while, those fingers never stopped. "I'm sure."

"Hettie," he said softly.

Her bottom lip caught between her teeth but then slipped out. She was getting close.

"Come for me, baby. I want to see you come."

Her lips parted, but no words came out. Climbing onto the bed, he crawled up next to her and pulled a hard, perky nipple out from beneath her black lace bra. Immediately he drew it into his mouth; a gasp snagged in her throat as he tugged. With his free hand he fished out the other breast and went to work on the nipple, tugging and pinching, twisting and tweaking. Her breathing was labored beneath him, and her eyes shut as her hips jerked off the bed into her palm. He closed his eyes and laved at her tight peak, but the gentle sound of smacking forced him to blink them open.

Dear freaking Christ, she was smacking her clit with the tips of her fingers while arousal practically poured out of her into a pool on the bed. Had she always gotten this wet? He couldn't remember. A few more smacks that seemed to mesmerize him, and she resumed her circles. Still in awe, he watched as her back bowed on the bed, a cry lurched in her throat and her hips jerked as she came undone. He latched back on to a nipple and tugged, enhancing her climax, giving her more of what she needed. Fuck, she was beautiful when she came, so feminine, so uninhibited.

He wanted a lot more of that before the night was over. He wanted a lot more of that for the rest of his life.

CHAPTER 7

Three orgasms in twenty minutes. What the hell was going on? And she'd touched herself, brought herself to climax in front of Gavin. She'd never done that in front of a man before in her life. But something in Heather (besides the scotch) had made her do it. As he'd slowly released the pearly buttons of his crisp white dress shirt to reveal a washboard stomach and pecs worthy of a billboard, her hand suddenly had a life of its own. And the way he'd responded, playing with her nipples, had been perfect, and the orgasm had rocked her world.

After that third climax, Heather slumped back into the pillows and closed her eyes. The scotch was working its way through her veins and had pooled in all the right places: her belly, her feet, her brain and her pussy. Everything was happy and pliant and in a well-earned state of blissful atrophy.

The mattress shifted next to her, but she didn't bother to open up her eyes. Seconds later, the same velvety softness from earlier swept up her cleft again. She mewled from the pleasure but went to move away.

"Not yet," she said lazily, not bothering to open her eyes. "Too sensitive."

He shifted again. "What would you like then? I'll do anything for you."

She let out a loud sigh, and a smile coasted across her face. "Hmm, tie me to the headboard, spank me hard and lick my ass." A giggle much too girlie for her liking bubbled up before she could stop it. She clapped a hand to her mouth, but that only made her giggles turn into a laugh. She hadn't even bothered to open her eyes. It'd been ages since she'd had this much to drink, and apparently good scotch dissolved the filter in her brain.

Silence reigned supreme in her bedroom until she was forced to open her eyes. Had he quietly gathered his clothes and left? No. He just sat there on the side of the bed staring at her as if she'd just told him she, too, was a billionaire and had also been to outer space.

"Just kidding?" she said hopefully, at an attempt to ease the sudden choking tension in the room.

"Were you?"

No.

"Yes."

"I don't believe you."

She couldn't get a read on him. Not a lip or eyebrow twitch. He just sat there, his baby blues piercing her soul and making her want to submit to him in every way. But she couldn't, at least not in every way. He could have her body, but he'd never have her heart again.

Sitting up, she met his gaze dead-on. "So what if I'm not? A lot has changed in ten years."

"Apparently."

Her back went ramrod-straight from his tone. Was he judging her? If so, he could get the fuck out now. She went to open her mouth and say as much, but he was on her and she was beneath him in seconds, her arms above her head and pinned tightly beneath his one big, strong hand. He wedged a knee between her legs and pressed down against her still swollen and tender clit. Unable to control herself or her urges, she ground her cleft against him.

He hovered above her, waiting for her eyes to focus on his. "Is that what you want?"

"Yes," she breathed. Her nipples could cut glass, and her belly was doing somersaults and cartwheels.

Without another word, he flipped her over onto her front and began organizing her body how he saw fit. Up on her knees, legs spread, arms out, so she balanced on her elbows, head down. He climbed down off the bed, and she heard him rummaging around in one of her drawers. Seconds later he was back and binding her hands together with one of her silk scarves, then to the headboard.

"Restraint hooks are underneath," she whispered, her heart threatening to leap out of her chest from how turned on she was.

He simply grunted. But he found them and secured her wrists properly.

She didn't have much time to wait before that diabolical tongue from earlier found her center and he thrust inside. "God," she murmured into the pillow.

Up and down, around and around he fucked her with his mouth, drank her down, lapped her up. And then there was a poke. A soft, curious, sensual poke. She clenched on instinct but didn't push away. He swept his tongue up between her cheeks, then circled her tight hole. She trembled on the mattress as the sensations swamped her.

So forbidden. So wrong, but oh so good.

Two fingers trailed between her cleft, gathering her wetness and drawing it up her crease. He plunged those fingers inside and with unerring accuracy found her G-spot.

"Fuck!" Heather cried. "Fuck."

She was on the edge again, so close she could practically taste the climax when his mouth stopped, pulled away and a harsh and painful smack landed dead center on her left butt cheek. She yelped from the surprise but also from the sting.

"Fuck." This time it came out as more of a groan.

Another spank, but on the right. All the while, those fingers inside her kept crooking and beckoning the climax forward. She pushed her ass up into the air as the sting slowly seeped away to be replaced with a beautiful blooming warmth. Two more strikes, quick as could be, came down, this time lower on each cheek, where her ass connected with her thigh. She flinched but didn't say anything. A trickle of arousal ran down her inner thigh as Gavin just continued to fuck her with his fingers, mixing up smacking her ass with licking it. One second it was pleasure, the next pain, until the heat of one slipped into the other and she couldn't stop the fire. One more spank, and his mouth was back on her. She broke with a strangled cry that quickly morphed into a sob as he took her back up to the top of the cliff, only to toss her right off. Squeezing herself around his fingers, she allowed the orgasm to spear her, sending shards of ecstasy careening through her body into every corner, awakening long-forgotten erogenous zones and nerve endings.

"Oh my God," she choked as her body continued to unravel and the pleasure took over. "Oh God." His fingers never ceased. They just kept pressing harder and harder on her G-spot until she felt like she needed to pee. The first orgasm hadn't even ended when a new one, a bigger one, an overwhelming one took shape and burst free like a thousand sticks of dynamite.

Words eluded her as sounds dissolved and her vision blurred. A man hadn't hit her G-spot in ages. And never this hard. Spots clouded her vision, and suddenly she tasted blood. She'd bitten her lip so hard she broke the skin.

One final glorious smack to her backside, and Gavin was up next to her head, releasing the restraints. When her wrists were free, he was back beside her hips, massaging her tender behind with his big, warm hands.

"Jesus, fuck, Hettie," he groaned, pushing his erection into the side of her thigh. "Since when?"

"Since when what?" she asked on a sigh as she pressed her buttocks into his palms, soaking up the attention.

He kissed each cheek, then continued to massage. "Since when have you liked it rough and kinky?"

Craning her neck around to face him, she smiled coyly. "A few years now, I guess. You?"

He nodded. "A few years."

She grinned back at him. "You're good at it."

"You're fucking perfect at it." She made to turn over onto her back, but he stopped her. "We're not done." A shiver blitzed down her spine. "Do you have any toys?"

"Yes."

"Where?"

"My nightstand drawer."

His eyes followed her gaze, and he moved to go open it but then paused and lunged at her, flipping her onto her back and pinning her in place. His mouth crashed down on to hers, and his tongue wedged its way inside, demanding access, taking from her what he wanted without quarter. She parted her lips and welcomed him in, meeting each rhapsodic swirl of his tongue with her own. His kisses stole the air clean out of her lungs and swamped her with longing. She met each plunge of his demanding tongue and sucked on it like she would his cock. He groaned into her mouth, realizing just how good it would feel to have her lips elsewhere. He felt so good, lying there on top of her, holding her in place, dominating her body and making it hum. She could get used to the pleasure, the security, the devotion.

But she wouldn't.

No.

Instead, she took what he was offering her now, pleasure, closure, and an apology. The breakup sex they never had. He'd be gone later tonight, and she'd never have to see him again. She quickly did what she could to wrap a mantle around her heart as his body lowered to hers and he pressed his weight down, pushing her into the mattress. As he made her feel more like a woman than she had in years, she carefully drew that protective shield around herself so that come morning, she wouldn't be once again full of heartache and missing the love of her life.

Finally, releasing her mouth, he gazed down at her. "I realized I hadn't kissed you yet." A wry smile tickled his mouth. "At least not *these* lips."

She grinned up at him and playfully batted her lashes. "You're still a great kisser."

Lurching off of her, he opened up her drawer. "So are you." His eyes fell to the contents of her drawer of debauchery. Slowly those cobalt orbs grew wide, and his smile stretched wider. Reaching inside, he pulled out one of her favorites, a vibrating butt plug. He hit the button, and the silicone diamond began to tremble. Heather's pussy clenched.

Continuing to reach inside, rummaging and making a hell of a lot of noise, he finally brought out another one of her favorites. A pearly white strand of anal beads. They were pea-sized at the tip but gradually grew larger near the loop at the base. She'd had that strand forever and loved it. With the right person and if the pull-out was timed just right, she detonated like an atomic bomb.

Gavin lifted an eyebrow. "Into ass-play?"

She grinned at him. "What do you think?"

"I think you've become a dirty little slut since I was last inside you." It was said with a big grin and a chuckle, so she knew he was kidding. Gavin's ability to dirty talk had always made Heather blush, but she loved it and knew he liked the new side of her he was uncovering.

"And you were a priest for these last ten years?" she said back.

"Nope."

That stung.

More rummaging in the drawer.

"What are these?" He pulled out a small clear box containing half a dozen blue silicone thimble-looking objects. Opening the box, he pulled one out and cocked his head to the side like a curious kitten.

Pushing herself up to sitting, Heather reached for the one from his hand, removed her bra completely and allowed her breasts to tumble free. "These," she started, grabbing a tender nipple and pulling it out, causing it to tighten and turn an even deeper red, "are nipple suctions. They can also be used on the clit. They draw blood to the area and make everything super sensitive." Like a pro she provided a demonstration and deftly secured one to her left nipple. Gavin watched in awe. He handed her another one, and she promptly suctioned the tiny cup to the other nipple, inhaling slightly when the suction took hold.

"And one more for your clit," he ordered, handing her one more.

With a knowing smile she took the third one from him, spread her legs and suctioned it to her clit. A gasp floated from her mouth and she shut her eyes from the intense pulling and pleasure the sucker already wielded.

"Fuck, that's hot," Gavin murmured, his voice hoarse as his eyes roamed her body.

Sliding back down to her back, she reached for him. "Fuck me, Gavin. You promised."

Snatching his pants off the floor, he pulled out a strip of condoms. She smiled inwardly at his preparation. She had a full box, too, but she liked that their heads were in the same place. Reaching for him again, she spread her legs wide.

"Fuck me, please."

Growling, he tore open the condom wrapper, sheathed himself in record time, then bounded onto the bed. He hovered above her, his big muscular arms bunching with the strain of his own weight as he supported his body. Heather's hips jerked off the mattress. A dull ache pulsed between her legs as her clit throbbed and swelled and her nipples grew more and more sensitive. Lowering himself, he angled his hips at the apex of her thighs. Their eyes met.

"I'm so sorry, Hettie. I'm sorry for everything. For the hell I put you through, for breaking up with you the way I did, for breaking up with you at all. And I plan to spend the rest of my life making it up to you."

Her legs wrapped around his hips and she bucked up, desperate for the ultimate impalement. Now was not the time to be pouring out heartfelt apologies and waxing poetic. Now was the time to fuck.

"Gavin," she ground out through gritted teeth. "Fucking fuck me already."

Fire ignited in those sapphire eyes. Conviction and passion ruled. He reared up, then slammed home. She let out a small *oof* from the impact, but, God, it felt good.

"So fucking tight," he moaned, his mouth finding her neck and immediately clamping down hard. He'd always loved her neck. In the beginning when they were kids, she'd had to use a lot of makeup to hide the hickeys and bite marks. She clenched her Kegel muscles and locked her ankles behind his back, meeting him thrust for thrust, feeling his ass cheeks flex each time he reamed hard into her.

Yes. This was what she wanted. She wanted the fucking. She wanted the breakup sex.

Her hands grappled around his back and she held on tight, letting her nails graze his muscular back and enjoying the moan of pleasure that emanated from deep in Gavin's throat. With each deep thrust, his pelvic bone smacked her suctioned clit and pleasure whipped into a froth inside her. The devastating pleasure he pounded into her with savage intent edged closer and closer to pain, all the sharper for the hair-thin line.

"Harder," she mewled, pulling on his shoulders, wanting him deeper.

He lifted his head from the crook of her neck and gazed down at her. Without saying a word, he pulled out, reared up, flipped her over, and she was back on her stomach. She watched his hand snag the strand of anal beads off the nightstand and a bottle of lube.

Fuck yes.

Slowly, gently, he fed the beads into her ass. She whimpered and moaned from how good they felt going in, knowing they'd feel a million times better coming out. She pushed her clit into the mattress and a shiver raced down to her toes. She wasn't going to last long.

Without wasting another second, Gavin was back inside her, slamming into her from behind and causing her nipples and clit to brush against the bed. She was getting it from every side, every place. Every major erogenous zone was being looked after.

"Fuck, Hettie. I won't last long."

Neither would she. This was orgasm number five, or was it six? And still, she was able to come with zero problems.

His teeth raked her shoulder blade before clamping down hard. All the while his hips pumped and pumped, hammering her hard into the mattress, forcing the headboard to bash against the wall.

"Come for me, baby," she crooned, squeezing her muscles around his length again, feeling him swell inside her. "God, you feel so good."

"Yes!" he said with what almost sounded like a roar. "Always, Hettie. Forever, Hettie. I love your sexy little cunt. Fuck, I want no condoms. I want to see my cum gush from your pussy lips as you come."

Oh God, the imagery, the naughtiness, it was too much. Yes, she wanted that too. She was clean and had an IUD. If he was clean, too, she couldn't say no.

"I'm clean," he managed through clenched teeth. He was holding on by barely a thread. "You on the pill and clean too?"

"Yes," she panted.

"Can I fuck you without a wrap?"

"Yes."

Without hesitation he pulled out one more time, tore off the condom, then slammed home. He came instantly. Teeth once again found her shoulder and dug in, practically breaking the skin. His breath was warm and uneven next to her ear as he poured himself inside her. She contracted her walls around him, milking him, drawing in every last drop. With a weighted sigh, he collapsed against her back for a brief moment to find his head again and some semblance of equilibrium. Her entire body hummed with the need for release. She didn't have to wait long before Gavin roughly flipped her over to her back, spread her legs wide and thrust two fingers inside her. He pumped, and he pumped, drawing out his cum at the same time he coaxed another orgasm from her. Heather brought her hands up and cupped her breasts. She slowly removed the suckers from her nipples, inhaling abruptly from the rush of pain and splash of cool air. Her eyes flew open in shock from how tender they'd become. It'd been a while since she'd used the suctions.

"Fuck, Hettie, you're so fucking sexy. Watching your creamy little cunt spill my load is the hottest thing ever." He flicked the suction cup on her clit. "Take it off or leave it on?"

She swallowed. "Take it off."

With a gentleness that startled her, he removed the sucker. More pain flooded her, and right between her legs. But it was good pain, a heated pain. In less than a second, his lips were on her, and he was sucking her clit into his mouth, swirling his tongue around the sensitive hood. His fingers fucked her hard and quick, demanding another release. Then she began to feel that divine pop, pop sensation. One, two, three … pause, tongue swirl, fingers pumping, four, five. Gavin's lips enclosed around her clit again. He sucked hard and she came harder.

Just as Heather bowed her back and gave in to the climax, Gavin slowly pulled on the beads.

Yes! He knew what he was doing. Pleasure soared through her body and out into her limbs, ricocheting around inside her like a pinball machine. Bright white lights flashed behind her closed eyelids, and her pulse thudded in her ears as the last and final bead withdrew. Satiated, sated and in complete bliss, she melted into the bed, ordering sleep to claim her.

But apparently, Gavin had other ideas.

"Fuck, baby. Seeing you come, seeing my cum flow from your pussy, I'm hard as fuck again." He levered himself over her, his cock notched at her hyper-sensitive core. "Once more. Then shower," Gavin said softly, hovering above her, his voice sounding muffled and distant even though he was right in front of her.

Her body betrayed her, and she spread her legs wide, welcoming him home.

Slowly, gently, sweetly he thrust home. Tears pricked the corners of her eyes, so she refused to open them. He was making love to her. It wasn't just fucking anymore. Gavin was making love to her the way he used to. His head dipped, and he took a nipple into his mouth. She arched against him, gasping from the pleasure as he sawed his teeth back and forth.

"You're close again, baby. I can feel it. Come for me." His voice was strained, but knowing she couldn't take any more rough sex, he kept the pace slow and steady. If anything, the languid strokes of his cock in her sensitive channel were more torturous than if he were going fast. The orgasm was building, and it was building hard.

"Oh, God!" she cried, her hands raking down his back and grabbing his clenching ass cheeks as the orgasm burst free and took her body, shaking it like a rag doll. Her nails dug into his flesh, feeling the muscular globes of his ass contract with each powerful pump. He stilled, stiffened, then sighed, once again collapsing against her with his full weight.

Not sure if she'd dozed off or not, Heather roused and blinked at the feeling of big strong hands lifting her up and cradling her to a hard chest. Closing her eyes again, she snuggled in tight against the warmth. He smelled incredible. He'd always smelled incredible.

She heard the light in her master bathroom flick on and was forced to open her eyes. Gavin stepped inside her big slate shower, shutting the glass doors behind them. Not bothering to put her down, he turned on the water.

"Shower, one more quick, sweet fuck in bed, and then I'll let you sleep. Sound good?"

She was too tired, too deep in loopy, lusty, post-orgasm dream world to truly comprehend what he was saying. So she nodded and smiled, then soaked up all the attention, allowing Gavin to wash her hair and bathe her.

By the time she was out of the shower, back in bed and crying out his name one final time as he lost himself inside her, Heather was tired and boneless. She simply climbed back into bed after peeing, huddled in tight to his furnace of a body and was asleep as soon as her head hit the pillow. Forgetting all about her original plans of kicking him out after she had her way with him, instead she thought, just before she drifted off, how nice it was to have his muscles wrapped around her again as she fell asleep.

CHAPTER 8

Gavin

Slipping out of Hettie's bed in the early morning, Gavin stretched before pulling on his boxer briefs. Holy fuck, what a night. His little Hettie was a kinky wildcat in the sack. Who'd have thought?

He slipped on his pants and shirt, then with one final glance at the naked woman tangled up in the sheets, ducked out the door.

"What the hell?" Hettie said a short while later, as she fought a big yawn and padded barefoot out into the kitchen, wrapped up in fluffy white robe. "Why are you still here?"

Glancing up from the counter, with a big grin and a wink, Gavin poured her a cup of coffee before sliding it across the island. "You still take a splash of milk and honey in your coffee?"

Wariness still in her eyes, she accepted the coffee with both hands, then brought it up beneath her nose. "What are you still doing here?" she asked again.

Her eyes made their way around the kitchen, taking in the scene. He had two big plates dished out, full of decadent breakfast favorites: lox with poached eggs on brioche with olives, tomatoes, capers and peppers. Fresh fruit. A bowl of quinoa done up like sweet breakfast oatmeal, with dried fruit, nuts and coconut milk. Mimosas in flutes. And, of course, as they always used to have when they had breakfast together, one bowl of Frosted Flakes with milk that they would share. Why? Because *They're Grrrreat!*

"Did you make this?"

He'd been quick to dispose of the bag from The Aroma Sisters, a hip and popular little breakfast joint not too far away. The place had great reviews online, a unique and enticing menu and, lo and behold, was run by his mother's friend's daughter and her friend. She was the executive chef and part owner. He'd called her up, placed an order and had it delivered in under an hour. The promise of a big tip to a starving-student busboy always made people "hop to it."

But as much as he would have loved to lay claim to such a masterpiece, he didn't want to start their second chance off with a lie, even a small one. With another smile, he pulled the big brown paper bag out of the recycling bin under the sink. "No, I ordered it from The Aroma Sisters."

Her eyes went wide as she took a sip of her coffee. "That place isn't cheap. I went there once for work. Pricey but good."

"So? I'm loaded, remember?" He wandered over to her small bistro table and began to set it. Linen napkins were rolled around what appeared to be expensive silverware. The restaurant had supplied everything: plates, cutlery, napkins, even the champagne flutes and champagne.

"Oh yeah," she muttered, averting her eyes. "I'd thought maybe I'd imagined that in my drunken state last night."

"Nope. Sorry, baby. Hate to break it to you, but we're rich."

"*We?*"

Choosing to ignore her question and address it later, he made sure that everything was in its rightful place on the table before making his way toward Heather. Damn, she looked cute. All bundled up in that big robe, her tiny frame buried beneath the soft terry cloth. Her eyes still held signs of fatigue from a long, hard night of fucking, and pillow creases marred her otherwise flawless complexion. Reaching for her hand, he led her over to the table.

"Sit, please."

She did as she was instructed, placing her coffee cup next to her mimosa. Gavin unfurled the cloth napkin and draped it over her lap before tucking in her chair. Once she was set, he took his own seat.

Her eyes still held an edge of wariness to them. One he'd noticed yesterday at the restaurant but that he watched slowly dissolve as the night went on, as he worshiped her body and showed her just how sorry he was, how much he'd missed her and wanted her back.

"Dig in," he offered, smiling wide even though butterflies the size of eagles were flying around in his belly.

She fixed him with a steely stare, not bothering to lift a fork. "Why. Are. You. Still.

Here?"

Gavin took a sip of his coffee, leaning back in his chair. "I want you back."

"Too bad. Not gonna happen."

"Then what was last night?"

She rolled her eyes. "Belated breakup sex. But it was obviously a terrible idea if you read more into it than what it was."

"Which was?" he prodded.

"Two people who haven't seen each other in a while, fucking."

He shook his head. Damn, she was feisty and so cute when riled. "It was more than that, and you know it." He popped a piece of melon into his mouth and chewed methodically. Swallowing, he went on, "I've been in town for a few days. I just bought five acres on Sammamish Lake. I intend to build a house."

Fire danced in those gorgeous brown eyes. "You're *moving* here?"

"I'd like to. I want you back. Remember that last summer before I moved back east? When we spent time at Sammamish Lake in Bellevue, saw an open house and wandered in, pretending to be interesting in buying. Only instead we ate the free snacks and had sex in an upstairs closet? Then we went and had dinner and made plans about one day buying a plot of land, building a house and raising a family on the lake. I want that, Hettie. I want it all."

She shook her head, closed her eyes and massaged her temples with her thumb and middle finger. Did she have a headache? If she wasn't a big drinker, he would probably guess yes. She'd put away *a lot* of scotch last night. His little Hettie had been a tiger in bed, and Gavin figured the scotch might have helped her get there. Or at the very least put up the blinders when it came to him. He wasn't so sure sober Hettie liked him as much as drunk Hettie did.

"Hettie, look at me."

"I told you not to call me that," she gritted out, not bothering to open her eyes or stop the massage.

"You'll always be Hettie to me."

Finally, those big eyes flashed open, but now they were filled with fury and conviction. She pushed herself up to standing, letting the cloth napkin tumble to the floor. "I am not *Hettie* to you anymore. You lost the right to call me that when you dumped me over the phone a week before Valentine's Day ten years ago. Last night was obviously a huge mistake, and one I will never make again. You think one night of sex means I want you back? Means I still love you? Means I want to build a house on the lake and have a family with you?" Scoffing, she rolled her eyes again and shook her head in disgust. "You've got a real high opinion of yourself there, Mr. Almost-a-Billionaire."

She pointed to the door. "Get out."

Slowly standing up and pushing out from the table, Gavin studied her. Gold flames danced in her eyes, and red dashed across her high cheekbones. But as hard as she was trying to remain strong, remain fearless, her lip trembled, and water built up in her eyes. She was a single thread, one lone brick away from snapping or crumbling. Either one would break his heart.

"Hettie," he cooed, approaching her with extreme caution. The way one might approach a timid deer. "Let's talk about this."

Her lip trembled more, and a lone tear darted down her cheek. Her raised hand shook as she continued to point at the door. "Out!"

"Hettie."

"Out!" she screamed. "You come here. Shake up my world and ask for a second chance. How dare you? I won't give you the chance to break my heart again, Gavin McAllister. Never again." More tears. All Gavin wanted to do was draw her into him and comfort her. Stroke her hair, whisper into her neck that he'd never break her heart again and everything was going to be okay.

All the strength she appeared to have left propelled her toward the front door.

With a hopeful heart, Gavin had gone and grabbed his overnight bag from his rental car that morning. It had a few changes of clothes, his tooth brush, shave kit, et cetera. She spied it next to the hall closet door, grabbed it, opened the door and heaved the bag out into the hallway.

"Hettie ... "

He stopped next to her, and his heart shattered from the look on her face. So fragile, yet trying to be so strong. He wanted to be her strength. Her rock. After what he'd put her through, and now just losing her father, the woman didn't need to be strong, she needed to grieve and feel the loss. But instead she stood there, fighting the tears, fighting the chokehold her throat had on her, her whole body shaking as it warded off the sobs, glaring at him and demanding he leave her alone.

He couldn't. He couldn't leave her in such a vulnerable state. He wouldn't.

He reached for her. "Hettie, I don't want to leave you like this."

With strength he had no idea she possessed, she grabbed him by the shoulder and shoved him into the hallway, slamming the door behind him and flipping the deadbolt.

Seconds later, he heard the crying. Wracking sobs tumbled through the thick oak door and out into the hallway. He knocked on the door. "Hettie, come on, baby. Open up."

"Go away!"

"I'm not leaving you, not like this. Not ever again."

Her heard a *slump* sound and pictured her crumpling to the floor against the door. He placed his back to the door and slid down too.

"I'm right here, Hettie. I'm not going anywhere, okay?"

Silence.

"I loved you from the moment I saw you, did you know that? You had your hair in a French braid down your back, a pen behind your ear, black restaurant apron on and those adorable little red Converse shoes with the white stars. You ignored me, and I loved you harder."

More silence.

"And the fact that you made me chase you. Made me earn your love, made me grow up and do something with my life just made me love you even more. I would never have earned that scholarship to Columbia if it wasn't for you and your family. I owe you, your mother, your dad, I owe you guys my life."

He paused, waiting for a sound of any kind.

He'd have heard her if she'd walked away. At least he knew she was listening.

He pressed on. "I want it all with you, Hettie: marriage, babies, the white picket fence around our house on the lake. We'll buy a boat, teach the kids to water ski. You can continue to work if you want to, or not. The nonprofit I'm opening is going to need a lead accountant and office manager. If you want the job, it's yours. I want what you want. I want you. I want the life we dreamed about when we were eighteen and hopelessly in love. Because I'm still hopelessly in love with you. I always have been. I was just too fucked up, too lost to realize that everything I need, everything I want, I already had."

"Do you own G-Mac, Incorporated?" Her voice was soft and quiet, filled with strain. But at least she was talking to him.

"Yes."

Shit. He'd hoped to keep what she was going to ask him next a secret. But she was smart, damn smart. That's one of the things he loved most about her, that big sexy brain of hers.

"You bought the building the restaurant is in." It wasn't a question. She knew it to be true. She was just seeking confirmation or trying to catch him in a lie.

"Yes." No sense lying. He'd kept tabs on her family over the years, and eventually he'd reached out to Eddie. Eddie hadn't said anything to him about it, but Gavin found out the company that owned the building and land the restaurant was on had upped the rent, and Eddie wasn't sure he could afford it. Upon further inquiry, the company had done that as a way to force Eddie to close so they could apply for a rezoning application and turn the plot of land into a condo-slash-multi-commercial building site, rather than just one single commercial site. So, instead, Gavin had purchased the building and plot of land with his holding company and kept Eddie's rent as it was. Eddie had called Gavin a few months later asking if he was G-Mac, Inc. Gavin had confided in him that he was, saying he didn't want to see the restaurant or the people who had changed his life go under or be forced to move. And now that he had the means, he was going to give back. Eddie had been upset at first, his pride bruised. But eventually he gave in and had thanked Gavin. His voice choked over the phone as he told Gavin how much he missed the boy he'd considered a son. It was that phone conversation that prompted Gavin to head to Tahiti to see Tate and really start to turn his life around.

"You broke three hearts when you ended things," she whispered through the door. "Not just mine. My parents loved you like a son."

A thick lump formed in the back of Gavin's throat, and the coffee in his stomach churned and roiled until he felt ill. "I know, and I'll never forgive myself."

"What makes you think this time will be any different?"

"Because I'm older, wiser, and it took losing the best thing that ever happened to me for me to realize that it *was* the best thing, the best person, that ever happened to me. Hettie, I will spend the rest of my life making it up to you if you'll let me. I will apologize every day if I have to."

Noise on the other side of the door had him lurching to his feet. The box in his pocket was burning a hole through the denim, and on impulse he fell to one knee, pulled out the box and waited for the door to open.

Hoped for the door to open.

The deadbolt flipped, the knob turned. Her face appeared through the crack, her eyes red-rimmed and puffy. But when she spied him there on the floor, the ring sparkling in the light from the hallway, those eyes went saucer-size.

"Heather Luisa Maria Caterina Alvarez." His mouth twitched. "*Hettie. My* Hettie. I was a moron, a jackass, a ... a terrible boyfriend, a terrible person to break up with you, let alone do it the way I did. I still don't deserve you, but I would like to be given the chance to one day deserve you. One day. If you'll let me. I want to share my life with you. Share in your hopes and dreams, your ups and your downs. I want to be your strength, your rock, the man you turn to when you need someone to just hold you, or when you need someone to help you fight your battles. I will be your sidekick, your enforcer, your companion. I will be whatever you need me to be. If you'll let me." His jaw ached from how hard he'd been fighting off the tremble and his own tears. But he needed to get it all out. He needed to win her back. If he didn't, he wasn't sure what he'd do. "Please, Hettie. Marry me and let me spend the rest of our lives trying to be the man you deserve, the man you *thought* I was all those years ago. The man you loved."

Her bottom lip quivered as she pushed the door open wider, still staring down at him with a mixed expression of shock, sadness, anger and—was that hope?

Gavin swallowed. "Will you marry me, Heather?"

A muscle ticked along her strong jaw. She wasn't blinking. Finally, she shook her head. "No."

Gavin's pulse picked up and spots clouded his vision as his whole world began to quake, the earth threatening to give out from under him.

"No. I won't marry you ... right now. But," she stepped back and brought the door with her, her other hand welcoming him inside. "But I will have breakfast with you. And will date you."

Gavin's eyes went wide, and he quickly scrambled to his feet and inside the apartment again.

Heather closed the door, turning to face him. "I don't know you anymore, Gavin. And I'm not agreeing to marry someone I don't know. But what I know so far, I like. I'd like to get to know the new Gavin McAllister, see if we have as much chemistry now as we did ten years ago."

His chest expanded and his grin spread achingly wide across his face. He nodded. "I'd like that, too. Can I take you out tonight?"

Wiping the back of her wrist beneath her eyes, Heather walked past him to the bistro table in her small dining room. She took a seat. He followed her and did the same, hesitation in his steps. At any minute she could have second thoughts and kick his ass to the curb.

"I'd like to go out with you tonight," she said, as she took a sip of her mimosa.

He heaved a sigh of sweet relief. "Dinner and a movie?"

"Sure."

Holy shit! He was going on a date with Heather Alvarez. This was almost better than her agreeing to marry him. Because now, he got to woo and court and seduce her all over again. He was friends with a couple of high-profile chefs in Seattle; maybe they could go and get dinner with tableside service. The cogs were spinning at warp speed in his head with new ways he could impress and wow her.

Heather started to cut into her breakfast. "You should know, though," she started. "I don't put out on the first date. I made my first boyfriend wait nearly six months before we had sex. And I've never slept with anyone before the third date."

Gavin smiled, feeling comfortable enough to dig into his own meal. "Poor bugger, six months, huh? You must have rocked his world, though?"

Her head was down as she ate, but a shoulder lifted and her lips tilted demurely. "He didn't last long, just a minute or two."

Gavin nearly choked on his oatmeal. "Shit. I bet it was because you're just that beautiful, he couldn't control himself."

"Perhaps." She lifted her head just slightly, but her eyes shifted upward and she stared at him, her gaze unwavering. "Two minutes or not, the guy was the love of my life. He hurt me, but I think I can forgive him. I think he's changed. And last night he proved he's not Mr. Two Minutes anymore. So, that's a plus."

Gavin's chest tightened. "A *huge* plus. But more importantly, you think you can forgive him?"

Meeting his gaze dead-on, she lifted her champagne flute. "I think I can. To starting over? I can't say I'll fall in love with you quickly, or that this road will be easy, but I'd like to try."

Love swelled inside of him as he lifted his own mimosa in the air to clink it with hers. "Take as long as you need, Hettie. I'm not going anywhere this time."

EPILOGUE

Epilogue

A year or so later ...

The door to the private jet opened to reveal a paradise Heather had never seen in her life—lush green hills, crystal blue water, and people standing on the tarmac wearing giant smiles and sunglasses.

They hadn't even put two feet, let alone four on the tarmac, before Gavin was crushed into a big bear hug by a tall man with green eyes, light brown hair and a sexy smile.

"There he is," Tate said with a chuckle, releasing his brother but holding on to Gavin's shoulders. "How do you feel? Nervous?"

Gavin rolled his eyes, but the grin on his face was a mile wide. "Excited for sure. I'm marrying the love of my life and on a tropical island no less. Nothing wrong with that." Heather snuggled in next to him. She couldn't agree more. There were no nerves coursing through her today. None. She was marrying the love of her life. Her family was with her. Everything was perfect.

A woman with long red hair, bright blue eyes, a baby on her hip and what appeared to be another one in her belly stepped forward. She immediately embraced Heather. "We've Skyped, so I feel like I know you. But it's nice to finally meet you in person."

Heather hugged her back, avoiding the swinging fists of the baby. "It's nice to finally meet you, too, Parker. And this must be Ellie. Wow, she looks just like her daddy."

Parker smiled wistfully and glanced at her husband. "I'm rather okay with that."

Heather matched Parker's grin. "I would be, too."

A man who looked similar to the brothers approached hesitantly. But when Tate caught him hovering in the shadow of the big plane wing, he quickly dashed over, looped his arm around the young guy's neck and brought him over. Heather didn't think he could be any more than around twenty-four or so.

Tate was still all smiles. "Guys, this is Warren."

Warren lifted his head, and the same blue eyes as Gavin's twinkled back. "Long-lost brother number three," he chuckled, toeing at a rock on the tarmac.

"Any word about our sister?" Gavin asked.

Tate shook his head. "Not yet. But we'll find her. I found you two, didn't I?"

Gavin frowned and nodded. Then he focused his gaze on Warren. "Nice to meet you, bro. Phone, Skype and email are nice, but I'm happy to know you're not taller than me."

Warren smiled back shyly. "You, too."

Gavin draped an arm around Heather's shoulders and tugged her in. "This here's my woman, Hettie. Is it too early to ask you and Tate to be my best men?"

Warren's eyes went wide. "Really?"

Gavin nodded. "Sure. We're getting married. Growing our family. Might as well start by making you part of the whole damn thing. You *are* family."

Warren's giant Adam's apple bobbed heavy in his throat. "I'd be honored."

Gavin grinned as he swung Heather up into his arms. "Perfect. Now that I've found myself a family and groomsmen, let's go get me and this gorgeous woman hitched. I'm tired of not being able to call her *wife*."

Heather giggled as she wrapped her arms around his neck and glanced back at her new family and the guests pouring out of the jet behind them. "Sounds like one hell of a plan!"

Grab the next book in the series here —> https://books2read.com/QReckless-QBS

If you've enjoyed this book, please consider leaving a review. It really does make a difference.
Thank you again.
Xoxo
Whitley Cox

<u>**DON'T FORGET!!!**</u>
Be sure to subscribe to my newsletter here: http://eepurl.com/ckh5yT
You'll get access to bonus content, deals, upcoming sales, giveaways, excerpts and all the latest news about my upcoming releases. I also sometimes post photos of our family adventures kayaking and camping.
No spam though because that's not cool. And I certainly don't share your email address with anybody but my dog and he's too busy forming grudges against dogs he's never me to do anything with your email address.

Sneak Peak from Quick & Reckless, Book 3, The Quick Billionaires
A Novel

<u>Chapter 1</u>

Silver

Stupid motherfucker. Selfish jackass. Prickless prick. If she ever saw that son of a bitch again, she'd rip his balls off with her bare hands and shove them down Candy's throat. Lord knows that home-wrecking slut had other parts of Silver's fiancé down her throat at some point.

Fuckers. Both of them. And they could rot in hell for all she cared.

Handing the cab driver a hundred dollar bill and not even bothering to get change, Silver stepped out of the taxi, slammed the door and made her way toward the wide double doors of the hotel bar. She'd asked the cabby to take her to a bar, far, far away from the church. To a place where she wouldn't run into anyone she knew and could just wallow, drink and forget. He'd nodded solemnly, taking in her state of dress and tear-stained face, and then driven roughly forty minutes out of West Vancouver and toward downtown.

The June weather was warm. Perfect wedding weather. Fuck weddings. Fuck grooms. Fuck commitment. Fuck life.

The hinges squealed as she heaved on the brass handle and pulled open the door. The bar was dark, but clean and inviting. There were no weird stains on the carpet, the smell of Lemon Pledge hung gently in the air, and the bartender appeared to have all his teeth and not be a lecherous weirdo. Things were looking up ... slightly.

It was a newer hotel, so everything still seemed shiny and fresh. Yet, even then, there was an Old World vibe to the place. A grand piano sat on a stage near the back along with a microphone stand, there were dark booths lining each of the walls, and all the lighting was muted and intimate. The perfect place to get lost in one's problems and not be noticed by a soul as the alcohol slowly numbed the pain. Dusk was setting in, so the outside patio seemed to be hopping, but inside was still rather quiet, and only a scattering of people rimmed the horseshoe bar.

Silver pulled up a stool at the bar. It wasn't lost on her that she was drawing a few glances. She was hard to miss. But she hadn't had time to run home and change. At least not to *their* home. She fought back tears.

I will not cry.

Their home. God. She couldn't live there anymore. Not with the knowledge that Trent had probably fucked Candy all over their goddamn apartment. Besides her clothes, Silver was going to have to burn the rest of her stuff, or at the very least disinfect the bejesus out of it.

She shuddered at the thought.

"What can I get you?"

Silver's head snapped up from where she'd been staring at the engagement ring on her finger to find the bartender, an attractive man in his mid- to later fifties, giving her the curious lone eyebrow quirk. "I'm guessing something hard and mind-numbing?"

Silver nodded. "Sounds perfect."

The bartender nodded back and walked away for a moment. He returned seconds later with a clean lowball glass and a bottle of what looked to be decent whiskey. He poured an ounce.

"More." Silver nodded, tapping the bar.

He added another ounce, then glanced up at her.

She nodded.

He poured.

When it was around four ounces she finally tapped the bar again. He sniffed through his nose and gave her a lopsided smile filled with sympathy before taking off to the other side of the bar.

Silver brought the glass to her lips and took a sip.

It burned.

She winced.

She took another sip.

It still burned.

But she liked the pain. It matched the pain in her heart. It matched the pain she wanted to inflict on Trent and Candy.

"People only drink like that for two reasons," said a deep and sexy voice with what sounded like an Australian accent. "They're either wallowing or celebrating. And I'm guessing right now," his eyes traveled the length her, climbing her body with such lazy indulgence you'd think she was naked, "you're the former."

Yes, definitely an Aussie. Her skin broke out into gooseflesh despite the warmth of the bar. She could have sworn she felt his hand travel up her arm. But he was several seats over, and both his hands were cradling his beer bottle.

"What gave it away?" she asked with a snort.

His smile stole the breath from her lungs, and she swayed where she sat. Glancing briefly at her glass, Silver contemplated another sip. Was she already drunk? Or was he just that handsome?

"You here alone?" she asked. Glancing at her glass again, she shrugged, tipped it back and drained it. This time both the bushy brows of the bartender lifted on his forehead. She nodded. He was over in a jiff, topping her up.

Aussie man chuckled. Fuck, even his laugh was sexy. Throaty and deep, and just rough enough to suggest he may at one point have enjoyed the odd cigarette or indulged in a weekly cigar. He was tucked just far enough away, near the dimly lit corner of the bar, so she couldn't quite tell how old he was or what color his eyes were. She knew his hair was dark, but if his eyes were blue, she was a goner.

"I'm here alone," he finally answered. "Why do you ask?"

Silver's eyes drifted to the vacant seat beside her. "I hate to drink alone," she said.

Taking her invitation, he moved over three seats and joined her. One of the pot lights overhead was shining down on him now, giving her the perfect opportunity to see every inch of his big, hard body.

He was younger than she would have thought, given the deep voice, maybe twenty-eight or thirty? But his face didn't hold an ounce of baby to it, it was all man. Chiseled and refined, with a dark, close-shaved scruff hugging his angular jaw.

His laugh stirred her from her scrutiny. "Ya done checking me out?"

Silver swallowed and removed her eyes from the V of his legs. Fuck, had she really been staring at the crotch of his dark-wash jeans? She was biting her lip, and her face was warm.

Yup, she had been.

Shit.

With embarrassment clinging to every cell of her body, she slowly lifted her head. *Double shit.*

Those were some blue eyes.

"Hmm?" he hummed.

Swallowing again, she nodded. "Uh-huh."

"Good."

She rolled her bottom lip between her teeth again. Could she? Should she? She'd never done a reckless or spontaneous thing in her life, and look where that got her. Sitting in a random hotel bar on her wedding night, contemplating asking a hot, sexy foreigner to fuck her brains out on what was *supposed* to be the happiest day of her life. Yep, if this wasn't rock bottom, Silver didn't know what was.

"You, ah, you staying at the hotel?" she asked, nerves running rampant through her at the idea of what she was doing. She'd never propositioned someone before; hell, she'd never even hit on a guy before. But just like a bolt of lightning, that whiskey hit her in the brain hard and then whooshed right down until her toes tingled. She could do this. She was *going* to do this. Tipping back her glass one more time, and with new whiskey-fueled confidence, she signaled for the bartender.

He was back in a flash. "Careful, Miss. I hope you intend to cab home."

"Cabbed here," she said, flashing him a big, drunk smile.

He nodded solemnly as he poured her two more ounces.

"So." She turned to face Mr. Sexy-Accent Man. "You staying upstairs? Got a room?"

His smile was slow and sexy, and the way it made every muscle inside her clench had Silver crossing her legs and squeezing before she knew what she was doing. "I don't fuck drunk chicks."

Her bottom lip dropped open. "I ... uh ... "

Reaching back down the bar closer to where he'd been sitting, he snatched a big leather menu off the top of a pile. "Pick something to eat. I'm buying. You need to put some food in your belly, otherwise you won't be able to walk, let alone talk or fuck in an hour."

"I ... uh ... "

He flipped open the menu and started perusing. "I could go for a burger. You?"

She hadn't even been thinking about food. After this afternoon, nothing but booze and lots of it had been on her mind. But then the more she thought about it, the more she realized she was starving. She'd been too nervous to eat this morning. Her aunt had said it was cold feet, the jitters, but now Silver thought perhaps it was intuition. That she knew, deep down, how the day was going to play out.

A burger sounded perfect. A greasy, gooey, cheesy burger with lots of fries. And onion rings. She didn't have to fit into a dress anymore, so she'd eat whatever she wanted.

She nodded. "Sounds perfect."

<u>**Acknowledgments**</u>

There are so many people to thank who have helped me on this daunting journey to becoming a published writer. First and foremost, my friend and editor Chris Kridler, you lady are a blessing, a gem and an all around amazing human being. Thank you for your honesty and hard work.

Jeanne St. James for doing the first beta-read for me, your notes, incite and ideas were so helpful. Thank you. Justine and Krista for their beta-read as well. I love that I can hand you the rough, unedited stuff and you'll read it and give me your feedback. Thank you.

Megan at EmCat Designs, your covers are fantastic, and you are a peach. Keep 'em coming, lady!

The Naughty Room Readers authors, I love being part of such a tremendous set of inspiring, talented and supportive women. Thank you for letting me learn, lean on and join the team.

My street team, Whitley Cox's Fabulously Filthy Readers, you are all awesome and I feel so blessed to have found such wonderful fans.

The ladies in Vancouver Island Romance Authors, your support and insight have been incredibly helpful, and I'm so honored to be apart of a group of such talented writers.

And lastly, of course, the husband. My rock, my travel companion, my partner in crime, my everything. I love you.

<u>About the Author</u>

A Canadian West Coast baby born and raised, Whitley is married to her high school sweetheart, and together they have two beautiful daughters and a fluffy dog. She spends her days making food that gets thrown on the floor, vacuuming Cheerios out from under the couch and making sure that the dog food doesn't end up in the air conditioner. But when the kids are in school, and it's not quite wine o'clock, Whitley sits down, avoids the pile of laundry on the couch, and writes. A lover of all things decadent; wine, cheese, chocolate and spicy erotic romance, Whitley brings the humorous side of sex, the ridiculous side of relationships and the suspense of everyday life into her stories. With single dads, firefighters, Navy SEALs, mommy wars, body issues, threesomes, bondage and role-playing, Whitley's books have all the funny and fabulously filthy words you could hope for.

True, Deep and Forever: Part 1
The Dark and Damaged Hearts Book 5

https://books2read.com/TDF1-DDH
Amy and Garrett
*

True, Deep and Forever: Part 2
The Dark and Damaged Hearts Book 6

https://books2read.com/TDF2-DDH
Amy and Garrett
*

Hard, Fast and Madly: Part 1
The Dark and Damaged Hearts Series Book 7

https://books2read.com/HFM1-DDH
Freya and Jacob
*

Hard, Fast and Madly: Part 2
The Dark and Damaged Hearts Series Book 8

https://books2read.com/HFM1-DDH
Freya and Jacob
*

<h2 style="text-align:center">THE QUICK BILLIONAIRES SERIES</h2>

Quick & Dirty
Book 1, A Quick Billionaires Novel

https://books2read.com/QDirty-QBS
Parker and Tate
*

Quick & Easy
Book 2, A Quick Billionaires Novella

https://books2read.com/QEasy-QBS

Heather and Gavin
*

Quick & Reckless
Book 3, A Quick Billionaires Novel

https://books2read.com/QReckless-QBS
Silver and Warren
*

Quick & Dangerous
Book 4, A Quick Billionaires Novel

https://books2read.com/QDangerous-QBS

Skyler and Roberto
*

Quick & Snowy
The Quick Billionaires, Book 5

https://books2read.com/QSnowy-QBS
Brier and Barnes
*

THE SINGLE DADS OF SEATTLE SERIES

Hired by the Single Dad

https://books2read.com/HBTSD-SDS
The Single Dads of Seattle, Book 1
Tori and Mark
*

Dancing with the Single Dad

https://books2read.com/DWTSD-SDS
The Single Dads of Seattle, Book 2
Violet and Adam
*

Saved by the Single Dad

https://books2read.com/SBTSD-SDS
The Single Dads of Seattle, Book 3
Paige and Mitch
*

Living with the Single Dad

https://books2read.com/LWTSD-SDS
The Single Dads of Seattle, Book 4
Isobel and Aaron
*

Christmas with the Single Dad

https://books2read.com/CWTSD-SDS
The Single Dads of Seattle, Book 5
Aurora and Zak
*

New Year's with the Single Dad

https://books2read.com/NYWTSD-SDS
The Single Dads of Seattle, Book 6
Zara and Emmett
*

Valentine's with the Single Dad

https://books2read.com/VWTSD-SDS
The Single Dads of Seattle, Book 7
Lowenna and Mason
*

Neighbors with the Single Dad

https://books2read.com/NWTSD-SDS
The Single Dads of Seattle, Book 8
Eva and Scott
*

Flirting with the Single Dad

The Single Dads of Seattle, Book 9
Tessa and Atlas
*

Falling for the Single Dad

https://books2read.com/FFTSD-SDS
The Single Dads of Seattle, Book 10
Liam and Richelle
*

THE SINGLE MOMS OF SEATTLE

Hot for Teacher

https://books2read.com/HFT-SMS
The Single Moms of Seattle, Book1
Celeste and Max
*

Hot for a Cop

https://books2read.com/HFAC-SMS
The Single Moms of Seattle, Book 2
Lauren and Isaac
*

Hot for the Handyman

https://books2read.com/HTHM-SMS
The Single Moms of Seattle, Book 3
Bianca and Jack
*

Mr. Gray Sweatpants
A Single Moms of Seattle spin-off book

https://books2read.com/MrGraySweatpants
Casey and Leo

THE HARTY BOYS

Hard Hart

https://books2read.com/HH-HB
The Harty Boys, Book 1
Krista and Brock
*

Lost Hart
The Harty Boys, Book 2

https://books2read.com/LH-HB
Stacey and Chase
*

Torn Hart
The Harty Boys, Book 3

https://books2read.com/THART-HB
Lydia and Rex
*

Dark Hart
The Harty Boys, Book 4

https://books2read.com/DH-HB
Pasha and Heath
*

Full Hart
The Harty Boys, Book 5

https://books2read.com/FH-HB
A Harty Boys Family Christmas
Joy and Grant

THE YOUNG SISTER SERIES

Not Over You
A Young Sisters Novel, Book 1

<u>WINTER HARBOR HEROES</u>

Co-Written with Ember Leigh

https://books2read.com/the-asshole-heir
Amaya and Carson
*

The Rebel Heir
Winter Harbor Heroes, Book 3

https://books2read.com/the-rebel-heir
Lily and Colton
*

The Matchmaking Heirs

First Winter Harbor Christmas

Winter Harbor Heroes, Book 4

https://books2read.com/the-matchmaking-heirs
Callum, Harlow, Carson, Amaya, Colton, Lily
*

THE SINGLE DADS OF SAN CAMANEZ: THE BREW BROTHERS

Rescued by the Single Dad
The Single Dads of San Camanez: The Brew Brothers, Book 1

https://books2read.com/RBTSD-BB-SDSC

Brooke and Clint
*

Summer with the Single Dad
The Single Dads of San Camanez: The Brew Brothers, Book 2

https://books2read.com/SWTSD-BB-SDSC
Justine and Bennett
*

Smitten with the Single Dad
The Single Dads of San Camanez: The Brew Brothers, Book 3

https://books2read.com/SMIT-BB-SDSC
Vica and Wyatt

*

Challenged by the Single Dad
The Single Dads of San Camanez: The Brew Brothers, Book 4

https://books2read.com/CBTSD-BB-SDSC
Chloe and Dom

*

<u>STANDALONE TITLES</u>

Doctor Smug

https://books2read.com/DoctorSmug
Daisy and Riley

*

Hot Dad

https://books2read.com/Hot-Dad
Harper and Sam

*

Snowed In & Set Up

https://books2read.com/SISU
Amber, Will, Juniper, Hunter, Rowen, Austin

*

Love to Hate You

https://books2read.com/Love2HateYou
Alex and Eli

*

Lust Abroad

https://books2read.com/Lust-Abroad
Piper and Derrick

FIND WHITLEY HERE

Website: WhitleyCox.com
Email: readers4wcox@gmail.com
Twitter: @WhitleyCoxBooks
Instagram: @CoxWhitley
TikTok: @AuthorWhitleyCox
Facebook : https://www.facebook.com/CoxWhitley/
Blog: https://whitleycox.com/fabulously-filthy-blog-page/

Exclusive Facebook Reader Group:
https://www.facebook.com/groups/234716323653592/
Booksprout: https://booksprout.co/author/994/whitley-cox
Bookbub: https://www.bookbub.com/authors/whitley-cox
Goodreads:
https://www.goodreads.com/author/show/16344419.Whitley_Cox
Subscribe to my newsletter here:
http://eepurl.com/ckh5yT

www.ingramcontent.com/pod-product-compliance
Lightning Source LLC
Chambersburg PA
CBHW060450160726
47992CB00003B/1168